T0132447

Doglegs

A tale of human imperfection and dogged intervention

ART NOVAK

iUniverse, Inc.
New York Bloomington

*This is a work of fiction. All of the characters, names, incidents,
organizations, and dialogue in this novel are either the products
of the author's imagination or are used fictitiously.*

iUniverse books may be ordered through booksellers or by contacting:

*iUniverse
1663 Liberty Drive
Bloomington, IN 47403
www.iuniverse.com
1-800-Authors (1-800-288-4677)*

*Because of the dynamic nature of the Internet, any Web addresses or
links contained in this book may have changed since publication and may
no longer be valid. The views expressed in this work are solely those of
the author and do not necessarily reflect the views of the publisher, and
the publisher hereby disclaims any responsibility for them.*

*ISBN: 978-1-4401-7536-7 (sc)
ISBN: 978-1-4401-7538-1 (hc)
ISBN: 978-1-4401-7537-4 (ebook)*

Printed in the United States of America

iUniverse rev. date: 11/16/09

Contents

To Pal, Arby, Bubba, Copper,
and the regulars (human and canine) who met in the woods
where Edina and St. Louis Park meet Minneapolis

Acknowledgments

Thanks to John Gaspard, Mike Mioduski, Jennifer Reis, Mark Bazil, Maureen Burke, Ken Ziegler, John Lowe, my brother Burton, daughter Lauren, and wife Margie. These people, whose opinions I value, read *Doglegs* prior to publication and made helpful comments and suggestions.

Also, thanks to Savannah College of Art and Design, for encouraging me to complete this book by awarding me a Presidential Fellowship.

Finally, I would like to recognize the contributions of this eclectic group: Joseph Duemer, Beth Norman Harris, David Foote, Mary Lou Weber, Craig Olson, Austin Scott, J. Allen Boone, Jerry Seinfeld, Rod Stewart, Sigmund Freud, Lindsay Hadley, and Doris Day.

"There are some simple truths ... and the dogs know what they are."

— Joseph Duemer

As the squirrel darted past, my nose quivered, generating shock waves that stood my hair on end. "I must capture that scent," I thought, "and make it my own." The longing enveloped me. The promise propelled me. My master's call was audible but unreal. The world outside was a blur. All that existed was the fleeing squirrel.

— S.O.S.

Chapter 1
Matt's Turn

"C'mon, Matt. Life is waiting. Let's go for it. The grand adventure begins—*now!*" With his eyes fixed on mine, he spoke clearly and persuasively.

OK, technically the only sound that passed through my dog's lips—er, black gum line—was *"Rrrrrrrooooof!!!"* But the urgency he put into it spoke volumes.

Maybe "canine" and "canny" come from the same root. Has history recorded a single, silver-tongued human who could motivate another with a single syllable the way S.O.S. did with his *"Rrrrrrrooooof!!!"*? He was tapping into something going on inside of me that morning.

At least that's my impression now. Back then, I simply chalked up his excitation to the goofiness of a mutt with questionable breeding. After all, why should S.O.S. be any more jazzed about going down to Doglegs Park on that Saturday than he was on Friday or Thursday? From one day to the next, his life was more-less the same.

But mine wasn't. As I look back on it now, S.O.S. was picking up on something I wasn't consciously aware of yet. I was coming into my "time." Prime time. Magic time. I was a romantic, I suppose. I don't suppose—I *was* one. And a central tenet in the faith of all romantics is the belief in a short season of heightened sensibilities. A season when things happen that change the course of your life forever.

Of course, sometimes you have to help the season along. So you put yourself in places where it will be likelier to find you. No place was more perfect than Doglegs Park. Two adjacent municipalities would probably never be able to fashion a Doglegs Park by working together. But geography and serendipity conspired to let them create it working independently. First, the suburb of Eden View built Eden View Park along its south border. Not to be outdone, the community to the south, Priorwood, put in Webster Field along its north border. Connecting these two parks was a long tract of relatively unscathed wilderness, a densely wooded area complete with hills and trails. Part of it belonged to Eden View, part to Priorwood. Because they had been squabbling about the boundaries for so long, the two suburbs finally decided the only solution was simply to do nothing and leave the place alone.

So we—the "Dog People"—moved in and made this confluence of woodland and parkland our own. We dubbed it Doglegs because, as you head toward Eden View Park, the main trail through the woods takes a 45° dogleg to the right, straightens out for a bit, then takes another 45° dogleg to the left.

How lucky was I—on this idyllic Saturday morning in early April—to be living in a small, rented house one block from Webster Field? From my living room window, I could see the edge of the woods. S.O.S., I'm sure, could smell them.

As he yanked me out the front doorway, his tail wagged so hard and fast against the door, it sounded like someone knocking. If I'd had a tail, it would have been wagging as well. My roommate Doug and his dog Shela were already down at Doglegs, and we couldn't wait to join them. And not just them. That was the thing about Doglegs. It was a community unto itself. There was a large group of "regulars," people who brought their dogs down once, twice, sometimes even three times a day. By sheer force of numbers, we held sway. Kids were no competition. Aside from playing their regularly scheduled Little League games, suburban kids in the early twenty-first century spent most of their leisure time in their bedrooms playing baseball video games on their PCs. Nature apparently did not feel altogether natural to them.

But it did to the Dog People. Doglegs sucked every one of us in, always in the same way. We'd start out coming down just cause it was a great place to let your dog run free. Then, as we'd get to know everyone, it became more than that. We'd start to love it as much for ourselves as for our dogs.

Doglegs was simultaneously a place to get away from it all and a place to connect with people. We all knew

3

each other, if not by name, by our dogs' names. And we liked each other. After all, we were Dog People. We easily could wile away an hour or more talking "dogs" or just observing them. We didn't have to get into business or politics or religion or any of the stuff that divides people. Dogs were our religion, Doglegs our temple. And Dog People took on some of the less sinister characteristics of a cult. There was this common bond. We knew something that "they"—the outsiders—didn't. There were things we could get from dogs that others couldn't. Things we could get nowhere else. Hard-to-articulate things.

S.O.S. had found me four-and-a-half years earlier, at a time in my life when I was lost, quite literally. A recent arrival in Boston, where I was about to start veterinary school, I accidentally boarded the Green Line trolley one rainy morning instead of the Orange. About the same time I noticed my mistake, I also noticed a very wet, very collarless young mutt prancing up and down the aisle of the trolley car. When I asked if it belonged to anyone, a woman shook her head and shrugged. "He got on at Brookline Village."

Next thing I knew, the future S.O.S. jumped up on the empty seat next to mine and did not budge. Possibly because I am one sick puppy myself, I instantly had the sensation that we were meant to be together. And I was certain he felt the same way. I met no resistance—from him or anyone else—when I gathered him up in my arms (he was lighter then) and disembarked at the very next stop. We made our way home together through the rain.

Both of my parents had passed away before I finished my schooling. But S.O.S. was there to share in my satisfaction. And when I moved back to Priorwood, landed a job, found the house with Doug, S.O.S. was there to take part in the excitement. That's the thing about a good dog—it's always there, but you never tire of having it around.

I once read a quote that has always stayed with me: "The art of being wise is the art of knowing what to overlook." If that's true, I guess dogs are wiser than you or I. S.O.S. overlooked plenty. For instance, if he'd linger too long over some wonderful scent in the bushes, he'd never hold a grudge when I'd tug at his leash and force him to move on. He couldn't reason, "Matt's tugging on the leash cause he's late for work." But I'm convinced he instinctively understood that I was operating on a different level. Not necessarily a better level, but a legitimate one nonetheless. So he overlooked the fact that my leashing policy didn't jibe with his own sense of right and wrong.

Human-to-human relationships don't work that way. Oh, sure, *intellectually* we may think, "I really don't feel like going shopping with her when this football game's on, but I'll do it anyway, because it's important to her." Instinctively, however, that tug on our leash is going to leave a wound, and the wound will fester. Deep down, we don't instinctively believe that another person has the right to make us move against our will.

But a dog sometimes does have that right. In fact, at that very moment, I didn't mind at all that S.O.S. was tugging mercilessly on the leash all the way to the park. I swear I could have plopped myself down on the street and he'd have dragged me all the way there—he the sled dog and I the sled.

For all I know, he could have had some Alaskan Malamute in his breeding. He was so hard to categorize that when I adopted him, the Humane Society wouldn't even venture a guess as to his bloodlines. He had American water spaniel ears, Dalmatian energy, Bernese bulk, and a tongue that was all his own. It seemed to protrude perpetually four inches outside his mouth and twirl around like a propeller when he ran, which was most anytime he saw anyone, human or canine. A big, lovable hulk of white with black spots, S.O.S. would come barreling into you out of pure friendliness, too simpleminded to realize he had the potential to crunch a few bones. When people who knew him saw him running towards them, they'd sometimes holler "S.O.S.," and I never knew for sure if they were greeting him or issuing a cry for help.

Actually, S.O.S. was his nickname. It stood for Son of Sam, because Sam was my dad's name, and my dad had died a few weeks before I'd found the dog. Doug told me 'Son of Sam' was a little sick, but I had no problem with it. "What's the big deal?" I argued. "It's a name, for God's sake." But after giving it a little more thought, I figured most of the civilized world would probably share Doug's point of view. I didn't want a name that would attach any stigma to my dog—or to me. So the moniker etched on his ID tag was "S.O.S."

We ran together across Webster Field, my two legs working twice as hard as his four. I let him off the leash when we approached the woods. The park patrol wouldn't bother you if you let your dog run free in the woods—it was sort of an unwritten law. Every so often someone would get ticketed for having an unleashed dog in Webster Field. But for the most part, we Dog People were careful not to abuse our privileges.

As soon as S.O.S. did his customary poop, in the customary place, I whipped out my plastic bag and scooped it up. This was another of the unwritten laws of Doglegs. *Thou shalt clean up thy fleabag's poop.* Deep down I guess we all believed that this domain was a fragile gift that would break if we didn't handle it with extreme care.

So there was a code we lived by. We had to keep a low profile. We made an effort to keep our dogs from bothering dogless visitors to Webster Field or Eden View Park. And if there was an incident, we apologized profusely. We didn't need anyone complaining to the Park Board. And we tried to keep the woods immaculate. It was a small price to pay for the blessings of Doglegs. If some teenagers had a late-night party, we cleaned up the empty beer cans the next morning. If we found a dead raccoon, we disposed of it. Some of the regulars would even bring extra bags down to the park and pick up the messes left by other people's dogs. I guess I was never that fanatical.

But I would dutifully carry S.O.S.'s bag to the nearest garbage can. Doglegs' renown apparently had spread far enough that various animal shelters donated garbage cans and distributed them around the woods for convenient turd disposal. Some of the regulars had worked out a system. One would take the liners out of the cans when they were full and replace them. Another would carry the full liner bag to a nearby dumpster. So the least I could do was be diligent about helping to fill those liners.

That's just what I was doing when a voice called out to me from down the path. "Hey, I thought that new dog food you put her on is supposed to make her poop less."

I smiled, as he knew I would. It was Ben Schallert, the hotshot attorney. Now I have strong reason to suspect that when Ben talks over a case with his associates, he has occasion to say "shit." A lot. Why, you might wonder, would someone use "shit" to describe various forms of aggravation—as in, "My client is giving me a lot of shit"—but revert back to using "poop" when describing honest-to-goodness shit? I guess it all came down to the Doglegs code. It was a happy, G-rated, Ozzie-and-Harriet world.

"It makes her poop *less*," I said. "It doesn't make her poopless." He chuckled, as I knew he would. I liked Ben. He was about five years older than I, more worldly, and successful enough that he was a homeowner instead of a home renter. But inequities like that never came between people in Doglegs Park. And it didn't occur to me that I might not have liked him quite so much outside our canine Camelot.

We both turned to see Ben's golden retriever, Justice, laying down a load of his own. "Need a bag?" I offered. But Ben's pocket was bulging with plastic bags. One of the fringe benefits of dog ownership is that you never have to think twice when the checkout person asks, "Paper or plastic?"

With a bagged palm, he scooped up Justice's poop "hot out of the oven" (as we called it) and with the finesse of someone who had fine-tuned their technique through daily repetition. Oh, the things we took pride in down at Doglegs.

Ben strolled over to the garbage can with his contribution. "Did you hear what Jerry Seinfeld said about Martians coming to our planet?" he asked. I shook my head, already smiling. "They see us being led around on chains by these four-legged creatures and toting around bags filled with their poop. Who would the Martians conclude is in charge on this planet, and who are the slaves?"

We both laughed. Doglegs came with the conversation built right in. Dog humor. Dog wisdom. Dog adventures. We all became instant "friends" with each other. The friendships generally ended where the trail ended. But that's what was so perfect. Camaraderie without commitment. Sociability without responsibility.

Ben was on his way out of the woods. We exchanged "have-a-good-ones," and I continued down the trail, easily settling into a Daniel Boone frame of mind. It was easy to forget that this pristine timberland was tucked away in the heart of the metro. The location made it all the more precious. I was living in the moment and feeling right at home soaking up the sights and sounds and smells of springtime in the springtime of my life.

My dog was already way out ahead of me. Beyond him in the distance, I could see maybe half a dozen regulars standing around in the central meeting place, a clearing in the woods at the end of the first dogleg. We all simply referred to this spot as the Clearing. Under the shade of the large birch tree there, everyone could comfortably watch their dogs playing together and comment endlessly on the peculiarities that made every one unique.

S.O.S. made his usual grand entrance. When he got close to the Clearing, he crouched down on his forelegs, resembling a runner at the start of a fifty-yard dash. But this runner couldn't wait for the starting gun to go off. After just five seconds spent sizing up the party of pooches before him, his tail—not to mention his tongue—was wagging so vigorously it seemed to create a jet stream that blasted him forward, smack into the midst of the dog pack. His playfulness was not to be denied. He seemed to energize the group, canine and homo sapiens alike.

This was a typical group for a Saturday morning. Greg was there with Hershey and Nestle, his two Chocolate Labs. If we Dog People were somewhat cult-like, you could probably say Greg was our spiritual leader. Whenever two dogs got into an altercation, Greg was there to break it up. When a thirsty dog needed water, Greg was there. When a lost dog needed finding, Greg was there. Come to think of it, Greg was almost always there. Up in that birch tree at the Clearing, he had actually installed a makeshift lookout tower. He would sometimes spend hours up there, while Hershey and Nestle took naps in the shade below. From his perch up above, Greg took pleasure in watching over Doglegs, making sure everything and everybody in it were okay. If he'd had kids, he'd have been the ideal scout troop leader. Fortunately for us, he just had dogs.

Greg was throwing a ball for Hershey and Nestle to chase as he talked with Molly, a young-at-heart, white-of-hair woman in her seventies. She owned seven small Yorkshire Terriers, so it didn't take us long to christen her and her brood Snow White and the Seven Arfs. When she walked them outside of the woods, she used seven leashes that she would braid together, apparently making it easier for her to hold all seven handles in one hand. The leashes branched out to the collars of the seven dogs, who trotted along together with a degree of synchronization a team of Clydesdales would envy. When she let them "run free," they hardly ran at all, preferring to stick close to her. Sometimes I had the impression they didn't even know when they were off the leash.

At first glance, you might have concluded that Molly was the Doglegs eccentric. But we were all a little eccentric. The Dog People loved and respected Molly. When she smiled, which was often, her whole face would light up and reflect all the beauty of years gone by. Her upbeat nature belied a deeply intuitive mind. Whenever our exchanges went beyond the pleasantries, I sensed a wisdom beyond her years, which is saying quite a lot.

Doug was there as promised. He stood with Tom, Riva, and Elaine. Tom and Riva were a thirtyish married couple with a "baby," a five-month-old golden retriever named Cora. Cora trotted up to greet me and immediately began to lick my outstretched palm. This dog never missed an opportunity to lick.

Elaine, a softhearted woman of Chinese descent, held a stick in her hand. Tugging at the other end of that stick was her equally softhearted Rottweiler/shepherd mix, Woodman. Murphy was the dog's original name, but Elaine changed it to Woodman when she discovered that she really didn't need a leash for him. With stick in hand, she could walk to the corners of the earth, and he would follow right along, pulling tenaciously with all the strength he could muster.

Woodman's second favorite thing was to find a long, downed branch—the bigger the better—and somehow manage to pick it up, leaves and all. Then he'd run off with it to the top of the nearest mound, plop himself down, and enjoy a good solitary chew. Elaine's boyfriend had bought Woodman the T-shirt he was wearing, imprinted with the slogan, *So many twigs. So little time.* Talk about your perfect gift.

As I took my place among the regulars, all eyes were focused on S.O.S. and Shela, who wasted no time resuming their ongoing wrestling match. Shela (rhymes with Ella) was named for her mix of shepherd and Lab ancestry. She had the floppy ears and playfulness of a Lab, but the tan markings on her mostly black coat were clearly shepherd. Sixty pounds of pure muscle, she still had a puppy's exuberance. And why not? At three-and-a-half years of age, she was—in dog-years—just twenty-five, a couple of years younger than Doug and I. And we still considered ourselves two young pups, full of life.

S.O.S. and Shela found the cool soil of the Clearing ideal for wrestling. Before long, they weren't playing on the soil but *in* it. Shela began digging fast and furiously in the hole she had started the summer before. Other dogs had helped maintain the hole, but—make no mistake—Shela was the prime caretaker. Digging for her was as therapeutic as tugging was for Woodman. With a little encouragement, she'd have dug her way to China.

When Shela had finally excavated a den big enough for two, S.O.S. jumped in with her. To everyone's amusement, they lay down in it together, snug as two bugs in a rug. They tried to wrestle, but the space was so tight they couldn't do much more than embrace.

"I haven't seen S.O.S. this frisky in ages," Greg called out.

"Sometimes he still likes to get in touch with his inner puppy," I explained.

"We all do," chimed in Snow White. "Dogs are just better at it than we are."

After ten minutes of conversation about the antics of puppy dogs, the latest toys available for them, and the dangers of swallowing toy parts, Doug and I set out along the short straightaway leading to the second dogleg. Shela and S.O.S. were quickly up ahead of us, exploring. We walked in silence. What was there to say? We had hiked this trail together at least a hundred times. And been friends at least a hundred years. We'd eaten lunch together in grade school. Walked our dogs together in junior high. Drove to school together in high school. Roomed together in college. Co-rented a home together for the past two-plus years. It was about as committed a relationship as two guys could have without being gay. And I'm sure people wondered about us.

But though we were cut from the same cloth, the friendship was less than idyllic. Love-hate, you might say. We were overly competitive with each other. I was his benchmark, and he was mine. We measured our self-worth by how much we could outshine the other.

In grade school, we raced each other to get in the lunch line first. In high school, we competed for Jennifer Miller, and both lost, possibly because we cared more about winning our competition than winning Jennifer. And as we matured, I regret to inform you, we hardly matured at all. Well, okay, if you were to pin me down, I'd have to say I matured a little bit more than Doug.

Also, I think I can objectively say that I was just a bit smarter than Doug, a bit funnier, a bit kinder, a bit more analytical, and a bit more objective. Of course, Doug would probably say the same things about himself. As far as physical appearance, the world would probably judge Doug better-looking in the conventional sense, but I've got to believe I'm more interesting looking. His nose is kind of upturned and girly; I've got a man's nose.

Finally, I broke the silence. "Who else have you seen out here today?" I asked.

"Nobody but the crowd we just left behind," Doug reported. "Oh, Ben came through with Justice."

Not the answer I was hoping for. "Yeah, I ran into them down by Webster."

"Justice would be a good name for that dog even if Ben wasn't a lawyer. He gives equal time to every dog here. Never hogs the tennis balls. He even seems to watch out for the submissive ones."

"Right, Doug, he does the name Justice."

Doug winced, as I'd seen him do a thousand times before. Even our punmanship was competitive, although I clearly had him there.

But enough of this silliness. The woods grew very thick along the second dogleg. We began climbing a gentle grade that ended at the top of a ridge. Doug and I sat down at the top, where we had a nice vista overlooking Eden View Park. Our dogs were off amusing themselves in the woods behind us.

It was sunny, the first warm day of spring. I lay back on the freshly mown grass as Doug started in on his favorite topic—his high school students. Doug taught history. His anecdotes were generally interesting. But just then I felt a tranquil wave of drowsiness washing over me, and I couldn't manage more than knee-jerk responses. Doug's narrative increasingly sounded like it was coming from a galaxy far, far away.

" ... So I ask the class, if you could be anybody in history, who would you want to be? And this kid Corey says, 'Hitler.'"

All I could manage was an absent-minded, "Uh-huh."

Doug continued. "I said, 'Why Hitler?'"

"Hitler?" I responded. I was vaguely aware that my reaction was a little late. But I was too tired—and Doug too wrapped up in his story—to care.

"So the kid says, 'Well, if I was Hitler, maybe I'd understand how he came to be the nut-case he was.'"

"Yeah."

"So we started talking about how he'd started out as this painter, and somewhere along the line, something happened."

"Uh-huh ..."

"Wkldlfk plaejbe eopd gksdf yk elpkwmf qmwflpwdo ... "

I must have dozed off for a minute or two. My memory of that moment is a little hazy. The last thing I remember for sure was a fly buzzing around my face. Shortly afterward, I either dreamed I saw a robin or opened my eyes momentarily and actually did see one, in the elm tree overhead. I remember thinking, "The first robin of spring and the first fly of spring—they've come out together."

My sojourn through the land between wakefulness and sleep ended abruptly with a piercing yelp. Instinctively, Doug and I leaped to our feet and raced back into the woods, in the direction of the sound. We didn't know whose dog it was—yelps tend to be pretty generic. S.O.S. quickly solved the mystery when he came trotting out of some bushes. He was treading gingerly on his left hind leg, leaving dots of blood in its wake. Shela had already come bounding out from another direction, clearly unaware of her buddy's accident.

I looked at S.O.S.'s paw and made a tourniquet with my handkerchief. "Let's take a look around," I said, motioning toward the bushes.

"Be my guest," said Doug. "I'll sit with S.O.S. up on the ridge for a minute, give the bleeding a chance to stop."

"Meetcha back up there." I followed the blood-drop trail through the bushes and poked around. Shela was with me, doing a lot of sniffing but finding nothing. Then, off to the right, I spotted some shards of glass from a Miller Lite bottle. "Goddam teenagers," I thought, forgetting how recently I had been one myself. I carefully picked up all the glass and deposited it in a receptacle on the way back to the ridge. Greg would've been proud of me.

When I got back up to the ridge, Doug was sitting against a tree, his legs stretched out in front of him. S.O.S. was nuzzled up against one leg, his chin resting comfortably just above Doug's knee. Doug's arm seemed equally at home along S.O.S.'s flank. "Hey, Doug," I called out, "don't move. I've got Norman Rockwell here, and he wants to paint this scene. Oh, never mind, Norman says it's a little too hokey even for him." If I hadn't been so sure of S.O.S.'s devotion to me, I actually might have felt a pang of jealousy. For a moment I wondered if my roommate might be even more of a Dog Person than I was. That couldn't be. After all, I was the veterinarian.

"There was broken glass down by those bushes," I announced, as I took a seat next to them. "We oughta put signs up around the woods or something." Doug nodded, but he was preoccupied. I realized that both he and S.O.S.

were staring intently at a large oak tree not more than thirty yards into Eden View Park.

"What's so interesting?" I asked.

"A white squirrel."

"Oh, I've seen 'em down here before."

"Not like this one."

I caught sight of it as it was leaping from branch to branch like a trapeze artist. It seemed unfazed by the fact that some of the branches shook mightily from the impact. Then it lunged like a knife to the trunk and clung there so effortlessly you'd have thought the bark was made of Velcro. The exhibitionist squirrel remained stationary for just a few seconds, then scurried down the trunk and disappeared into the woods as if it were being chased. Well, it *was* being chased. While Doug restrained S.O.S., Shela lit out after it. She was smart enough to know she didn't stand a chance and quickly turned back, tail at half-mast.

"Squirrels must go into heat or something in the spring," Doug observed.

"Either that, or white squirrels are a little squirrelier than gray ones," I shrugged.

Seeing the tennis ball in Doug's hand, I figured we'd have to play at least one round of our game. Yeah, Doug and I had our own game, which we'd play only with each other. It developed out of the fun we'd had through the years watching our various dogs chase after tennis balls in various parks. So we decided *we* would chase tennis balls.

Yes, it was a little stupid.

17

I put the dogs on their leashes and tied them around a couple of nearby tree trunks. We couldn't allow the dogs to join in our game, cause they would always win.

"Alright, Doug. I'm ready." He hurled the ball, and we lit out after it, both hell-bent on victory. We shoved each other as we ran, neck and neck all the way. I was able to scoop up the ball first while on the run, but I didn't get a solid grip on it, and when it dropped, Doug pounced on it.

"I think that makes three in a row for me, doesn't it?" Doug wondered. "But who's counting?"

"Well, you're not gonna make it four in a row—not today at least. I'm gonna take S.O.S. home and wash out his cut."

"I'll make you a deal. If you want to stay here and get Shela nice and tired out, I'll take S.O.S. home. I've got papers to grade."

"Fair enough."

Doug handed me Shela's old tennis ball and trudged off. S.O.S. and Shela were a little confused about who was going with whom. Well-loved dogs never forget who they come in with.

To distract Shela, I tossed the munged-on ball down the hill into Eden View. The munger took off after it like a bat out of hell. I think, when a ball is moving, dogs believe it is a living thing.

When she caught up with her prize, she lay down with it for a moment, then decided it would be more fun to chase it again. She came over and dropped it at my feet. No sooner had I picked it up than she began whining for it. Apparently, its fresh deposit of saliva had increased its value in her eyes—or in her nose. I hurled it a long way, considering I was operating sitting down.

Just as Shela began chasing it, another dog came darting out of the woods, equally intent on the runaway ball. When I saw it was a springer-Brittany mix, I felt a pleasant twinge. Not that I have a thing for spaniels. But this spaniel's name was Mobile. I knew the dog's owner. And I knew that, in a matter of seconds, I could be seeing her, talking to her, getting to know her better.

I already mentioned that, if I'd been a dog, my tail would have been wagging when I left the house that morning. Now I may have led you to believe that it was simply the bright April morning and the beauty of Doglegs that had had me so revved up. And all that certainly played a part. But to be honest with you, I think, at some level, I'd known all along that the main reason for my sense of anticipation was the creature who was about to appear. In fact, it became very clear to me during those few seconds I waited for her—that eternity between the time she made her presence felt and the time she made it known.

Although I'm sure my gaze was fixed on the dogs, I couldn't tell you what they were doing. I saw nothing. And I wouldn't so much as turn my head to look up the path. I wanted Emily to speak first. Before my own actions influenced her in any way, I wanted to hear what sort of greeting she felt I was worthy of. She graciously complied.

"Oh, hi Matt ... It's 'Matt,' right? But where's S.O.S.?"

That voice. I'd only known Emily for about six weeks, yet somehow hers was the voice I had always heard in my head—such is the curse of the romantic. She had the faintest hint of an Irish lilt to her voice and smiling, Irish eyes. Most guys are T & A guys. I'm a V & E guy. Voice and eyes. Emily's eyes worked in tandem with her voice the way Fred Astaire's feet worked with music. Her words were expressive—almost musical—but totally without guile. And when she talked, her deep-set hazel eyes reflected every nuance. They too spoke eloquently, even more so when her voice fell silent.

Before that morning, I had seen her only three or four times, always at the Clearing, always with several other dog owners present. Each time we had talked casually. Each time she had attracted me more than the time before. But with other Dog People around, I'd felt too awkward to take our conversation beyond the usual pleasantries. The group dynamic at Doglegs made it hard to talk about anything but dogs. Today would be different. Today would be one-on-one, a whole new ball game.

That—plus the fact that her voice suddenly seemed so familiar—took away some of my nervousness. I was able to summon up my best nonchalant attitude.

"Oh, hi Emily. I've got my roommate's dog for the moment, and he's got mine. Why don't you pull up a ... hill?" I knew she'd be the kind of person who wouldn't mind sitting on a hill, even if the grass was still a little dewy. She wore jeans and a sweatshirt. And, at least to my unschooled eye, no makeup. Her hair was pulled back in a ponytail. On a face like that, why cover anything up?

So next thing I knew, there we were, just like that, sitting side by side on a hill, watching the dogs wrestling and trying to wrest a tennis ball from each other's mouths. Doglegs was making it happen.

"Love is in the air, wouldn't you say?" Emily remarked.

"Huh?"

Without looking at me, she motioned over to the dogs. They were lip-locked around the ball, Shela clinging to one half, Mobile to the other. I laughed, relieved and disappointed at the same time.

"Oh ... yeah. They're both after one thing."

"It must be great to have that freedom, huh? To know what you want and just go for it?"

"I think people are capable of being that straightforward."

"Really?" She said it in a skeptical, challenging way. "For instance?" Now I felt like *she* was throwing the ball, and I decided to go after it.

"For instance, I'd like to know if you've got any plans for tonight, cause if you're not doing anything special, we could maybe get dinner somewhere—without the dogs."

"Oh, *without* the dogs?" she sighed in mock disappointment. Then she quickly got serious. "Alright. What time?"

My instincts were right. This was my kind of girl. No phony enthusiasm and no coy hemming or hawing. Just a straight-to-the-point, "What time?"

"Say seven?"

"OK ... 'seven.' I better give you my address. I don't s'pose you have a pen on you?"

I shook my head. "Are you in the book?"

She shook *her* head, then held up a forefinger that told me she had an idea. "Mo," she called in her sweetest voice, "come here. Look what I've got for you." Mobile immediately conceded possession of the tennis ball to

21

Shela and, in abject obedience, came loping over to us. Emily's voice could charm the birds out of the trees. Of course, the piece of dog biscuit she held out to Mo didn't hurt either.

While Mobile munched on the treat, Emily removed the dog's collar and handed it to me. "My address and phone are on the tag," she said, matter-of-factly. "You can just bring the collar with you tonight."

"What's Mo gonna use in the meantime?"

"Can't we just trade collars 'til tonight?"

Trade collars?!! Considering this was someone I was just getting to know, it seemed like a pretty intimate transaction. Even though she was only getting my friend's dog's collar, I have to say it turned me on.

Using my sweetest, most persuasive shout, I called, "Shela, come!" Shela looked up momentarily, gave me a fleeting, defiant glance, then resumed her ball munging. "Shela," I repeated, "get over here—now!"

This time she didn't even bother looking up. So, much to my embarrassment and Emily's amusement, I spent the next few minutes chasing, cajoling, and pleading with Doug's fugitive hound. Then Emily called her once with open arms and Shela darted right up the hill to where she and Mo were sitting. By the time I got there, Emily had already switched the collars.

"I'm impressed," I said. "I had no idea I'd be having dinner with an actual Dog Whisperer."

She laughed easily, naturally. "Wanna know my secret?" She paused, wearing an impish smile. "Pure luck."

"I feel kind of lucky today, too." There was an awkward pause. "Well, a pleasure doing business with you, Miss

... Larkin," I said, searching out the name on the tag Shela now wore. I extended my hand for a businesslike handshake and wound up pulling Emily onto her feet. "You walking in the woods?" I asked.

"Sure. Let's go."

I kind of wished I had just said, "See you tonight," and gone on my way. It had all seemed so smooth, so storybook perfect, to that point. I wanted to spend the afternoon letting the magic build by reliving the morning in our minds. My usual modus operandi had been to live in the past or in the future. Suddenly I was living in the moment. It was a more alive feeling than I was accustomed to—an almost too-intense sensation.

But as soon as we started our stroll through the woods together, I felt at ease again. At first, we walked without a word. Words didn't seem necessary. On this remarkable day, it was enough to soak in the scenery.

We hiked single-file along a narrow side-trail that roughly paralleled the doglegs but meandered in whichever direction the foliage allowed. Whether it was my imagination working overtime or my intuition, I don't know, but there was something about the way she walked just behind me, matching me step for step, that made me feel this woman might accompany me to the ends of the earth.

As the widening path allowed us to walk side-by-side, the conversation opened up as well. All at once a torrent of words started flowing back and forth as we flawlessly executed the essential information dump on each other.

I can't speak for Emily, but I retained every shred of information offered. She was an assistant to the curator at the art museum, easy to remember because ... classy woman, classy job. She had two older sisters, which stuck in my mind, because I had two older brothers. And she had a dog-loving, sixteen-year-old niece, Iris, which I wasn't about to forget, seeing as how Emily mentioned her three times in the space of five minutes. I found myself envying this sixteen-year-old for the enthusiasm in Emily's voice whenever she talked about her.

"Oh, Iris, she's *not* a dog-lover, either. She's just like I was when I was that age—totally devoted to them. And my sister's condo doesn't allow dogs. So Iris is over at my place to play with Mobile every chance she gets. The backyard's fenced in, and they're out there together constantly. I'm afraid I'm gonna get kicked out of my apartment."

"Why?"

"Isn't it obvious?" she replied, motioning over to Mobile. At that moment, his front paws were working overtime, scooping out mounds of dirt and sending it flying into a pile behind him. His affinity for digging left little doubt that Shela had found her soulmate. "The dog *doesn't* like to dig." Emily smiled.

I was beginning to notice that she had an endearingly sarcastic way of saying the opposite of what she meant, when what she meant was so undeniable that saying it was superfluous. I was beginning to notice a lot of things about Emily. All of them endearing.

She slipped the leash on her dog while he was still digging. Then, despite considerable reluctance on Mobile's part, Emily managed to get him back onto the trail and into a sniffing mode.

When we got to the north end of Doglegs, we went our separate ways. She turned back toward Eden View, I headed across Webster Field. Through a monumental act of willpower, I thwarted a powerful impulse to leap into the air.

I reveled in the passion that permeated the room. The infectiousness of my mistress's joy enveloped me. The easy familiarity in the humans' voices inspired me. I nudged the dog that belonged to the one who was the source of my mistress's joy, and we wrestled with abandon. All barriers fell away. Yet something was not quite right.

— Mobile

Chapter 2
Doug's Turn

The best times in life generally aren't planned or anticipated. They just happen. It happened on the Friday afternoon Emily, Mobile, and Emily's niece paid Matt and I a surprise visit.

Almost three weeks had passed since Matt's first big date with Emily. That highly anticipated evening fizzled. He told me that at first he and Emily felt a little strange seeing each other in such an intimate way. By "intimate," he didn't mean they got naked or anything, just that, for the first time, they were seeing each other stripped of the security blanket that was Doglegs. By the time the awkwardness started to lift, Matt became nauseous, apparently the result of a shrimp cocktail he'd had at dinner. He managed to drop Emily off at her door and make it back to the curb for the first act of an all-night barfing extravaganza. But the fledgling relationship survived that inauspicious night. A little vomit was not about to extinguish the fire that had started blazing. For the next two weeks, they fanned the flames considerably. Then Emily's job took her out of town for the week, which fanned them even more. A lot of pent-up feeling was ready to explode by Friday, when Emily showed up unannounced with Mo and Iris.

This was also the first time I really saw Emily. Oh, I had seen her down at the park a few times. We'd had a sort of nodding acquaintance. But that Friday was the first time I really *saw* her. Never underestimate the influence of a best friend. For the past three weeks, I had seen and heard how Emily's presence in Matt's life had made him insufferably happy. Matt was flush with feeling for this woman. I—according to just about everyone I knew—was Matt's clone. I had been living this Emily thing vicariously through Matt. So I was primed to feel something. Until that Friday, what I had felt was a little jealous. But starting that Friday, a change would come over me. I'd feel a lot jealous. Emily marched right through the door and into my heart.

That wasn't the only surprise that afternoon. Emily's niece was instantly familiar.

"Iris?"

"Mr. Jesperson?!"

Iris Mohr was my brightest student. But that was only part of the reason she made third-hour my favorite class.

Above all, Iris was precociously clever. Sixteen going on forty.

"OhmyGod! *You're* Matt's roommate?!" she exclaimed.

"*You're* Mr. Jesperson, my favorite relative's favorite teacher?" added a beaming Emily.

"Just who the hell are you, Doug?" Matt challenged, totally straight-faced.

"Does this mean I can call you 'Doug?'" teased Iris.

"Not in class."

She tossed back a strand of jet-black hair, and her green eyes darted around our living room. "This is going to be a little weird for both of us, isn't it, Doug baby?"

"What are the odds?"

"It's got to rank right up there with Adams and Jefferson dying on the same day."

"Good historical reference."

"You've taught me well, Mr. ... Douggie."

The easy familiarity between my star pupil and me had Emily and Matt staring at us with equal parts amusement and amazement. But only for a moment. They quickly refocused their attention on each other. If anyone doubted the truthfulness of "Absence makes the heart grow fonder," they had only to observe these two. I'd say the palpable chemistry between them made me happy for my best friend. I'd say it if I could. But I'm only human. I didn't let it get to me though. I resolved to just be cool and join in the general merriment generated by three unruly dogs and four unabashed dog-lovers.

"Did you miss me?" Emily asked Matt, with just the right hint of coquettishness.

"Only when I thought about you."

"And how often was that?"

He gave her a peck on the lips, which apparently answered the question to her satisfaction.

"Aw, look ... Mo and S.O.S. missed each other too," observed Iris.

We all looked down to see the two engaged in a wrestling match. Ivory-studded mouths gnawed playfully at each other's necks as the dogs weaved and parried, pawed one other, and, at one point, seemed to embrace. Shela stood on the sidelines barking incessantly. Three could not play the wrestling game.

In order to stop the barking, I picked up a stick that S.O.S. had brought into the house and dangled it in front of Shela. She took the bait. Next thing we knew, Shela and S.O.S. were clinging tenaciously to opposite ends of the stick and thrashing about in a tug-of-war that would have done Woodman proud.

Now it was Mobile's turn to feel left out. Even though he'd been fixed, he leaped onto Shela's back and starting humping her. It was quite a show, two dogs engaged in a tug-of-war and two dogs engaged in pseudo-sex, yet only three dogs total. We had witnessed similar spectacles many times down at Doglegs, but never in our own living room.

Matt wrested the stick away from S.O.S. and Shela, and S.O.S. took the opportunity to resume his wrestling match with Mo. "They sure seem to like each other," Emily remarked.

"Oh yeah, you think wrestling is a sign of affection?" challenged Matt. With that, he picked Emily up in his arms, took her down to the floor, and began grappling with her. Emily was laughing too hard to provide much competition, unless you consider a caress of the neck a wrestling move. It soon degenerated into a tickling match, and now Emily was able to give as good as she got. I wouldn't have been surprised if someone had accidentally peed—and I'm not talking about the dogs. But it wouldn't have dampened anyone's spirits.

As she witnessed the early bloom of love between my friend and her aunt, Iris seemed fascinated. Watching her watching them, I saw in those flashing eyes the all-knowing wisdom of an old soul coexisting with the awestruck fascination of an adolescent. What she was observing, I knew, was the sort of intense relationship that would one day be hers. It was her birthright. She was as special as Emily, and I felt privileged to be someone she both liked and respected.

With Emily and Matt rolling about on the floor like a couple of lion cubs, and Mo and S.O.S. similarly engaged next to them, Iris and I—relatively sedate spectators on the sofa—started to feel a little self-conscious. She picked up on it right when I did.

"If you weren't my teacher, Mr. Jesperson, you and I could wrestle around on the floor too."

"But I *am* your teacher."

"Yeah. And if you laid a finger on me, I would sue."

So I did about the only thing I could do under the circumstances. I wrestled with Shela.

Then Matt brought out an unopened can of tennis balls, and I knew instantly what that meant. "Tennis-ball game!" he announced. "Virgin rules!"

"Huh?" said Iris.

I explained. "It's a little game Matt and I invented where we go after tennis balls like dogs."

"Okay. And just where does the virgin come in?" asked Emily.

"Oh, virgin *balls*," said Matt. "When we play with new tennis balls, the rules change. To win the game, instead of just getting your hands on the ball, you actually have to get it in your mouth, without using your hands."

Emily gave Iris a roll of the eyes that said, "Boys will be boys." "Okay, this I've gotta see."

Because "virgin rules" carries an increased risk of head collision, Matt and I put on our old football helmets. Then we all went out to the backyard. All except the dogs. If they came out back with us, they'd doubtless want to get into the game, and, needless to say, they would win every time. The noble tradition of the tennis-ball chase belongs to the canines as surely as the 3000-meter steeplechase belongs to the Kenyans.

In the first match-up, I went "head-to-head" against Matt. I got the jump on Emily's toss and managed to reach the ball first, kicking it off to the right, then pouncing on it with my mouth. Matt knew he was beaten and didn't even make the dive.

We let Iris and Emily put on the helmets and have a chance next. Matt and I watched in amazement as they both dove for the ball. Iris got to it first and actually had the ball in her mouth for a second, but it dribbled out, and Emily was waiting with open jaws.

"Well, Emily and I won our respective divisions," I announced. "So I guess we need to battle it out for the championship."

"Oh no you don't," said Matt. "She's mine." With that, he deposited the remaining virgin ball in my hand and ordered me to throw. Somewhat predictably, Matt and

31

Emily wound up in a lip-lock over the ball, and I declared the match a draw.

With the trio of barking dogs at the back window growing increasingly insistent, we let them outside to show us how the game is properly played. After we finally went back inside, our visitors stayed another all-too-quick hour. Matt regaled them with true-life veterinary tales. I made popcorn. Iris tossed kernels to the three dogs, who jockeyed for position like bridesmaids preparing for the bouquet toss. Because Iris and I were present, Matt and Emily tried their damnedest to keep their hands and eyes off of each other, but the gravitational pull was too great.

That night Matt was scheduled to work at an emergency veterinary clinic. So he and Emily, forced to spend another night apart, engaged in a nauseatingly protracted goodbye. With a wink and a nudge, Iris and I turned away and pretended not to notice.

We heard Emily say, "The Clearing in the morning."

"Ten o'clock sharp," promised Matt.

"And I'm *not* looking forward to it."

❋ ❋ ❋

After they left and before Matt went to work, he sat down at our desk and started scribbling. Something about the way he went about it told me he didn't want to be disturbed. Later that night, when Matt had gone, my curiosity got the best of me.

Not finding what I was looking for on the desk itself, I opened the top desk drawer. Tucked in a corner was a folded piece of paper. Carefully, but with feigned indifference, I opened it, all the while vaguely aware of feeling like the contemptible snoop that I was.

That feeling grew as I read:

To Emily from Matt,
You will never have to try with me
There is no way you could ever lie to me
Every word you speak will always sound like you
Every look you give will always look like you
Every move you make will always move like you
Every touch you give will always come from you
Every thought will live inside the heart of you
Every thing you do will be a part of you

Oh, the freedom. As I scampered down the street, the customary pressure round my neck was absent. Now my master ran at my side. The pull of Doglegs propelled him forward and rendered his tug on my leash unnecessary. The magic woman who waited in the woods brought forth a dog-like exuberance in him that had been lying dormant.

— S.O.S.

Chapter 3
Matt's Turn

Saturday morning found me in such a rush to get down to Doglegs, I think I was actually pulling S.O.S. instead of the other way round. I could imagine Emily hurrying toward the woods from the opposite direction, every step bringing her closer. In a matter of minutes, I once again would have to pretend that I was merely peering into someone's eyes instead of the windows to an angelic soul, simply listening to someone's words rather than music sweeter than any yet recorded. Of course, I knew she'd see right through me, yet respect my Herculean effort to keep my cool. Oh, I'm fully aware of how sappy I sound. Sappy, but sincere. And knowing she was feeling all the same things had me close to hyperventilating. This was not going to be one of those tragic unrequited love affairs. No sir. That last Saturday in April was made to order. Bright sun. Wispy clouds. The unmistakable aroma of early buds. And a cool breeze to keep the bugs at bay. On the path to the Clearing, I met Woodman, bounding along with—surprise, surprise—a huge tree limb. Two other dogs were right behind him giving chase. As Woodman passed me, the end of the limb banged into my leg. I grabbed the end of it and started pulling, amazed by the force Woodman exerted in the opposite direction.

"Are you okay?" Elaine asked, as she came up the path with the other dogs' owners. "He's dangerous when he starts running with those long branches."

"Oh, I'm fine." And I was. If I wasn't, I still would have said I was. It was part of the Doglegs Code of Conduct. You come down there with your dog and you tacitly agree to accept, as gracefully as possible, whatever Fate throws your way.

Even if the stick had caused significant damage, I think the pain would have been forgotten as the Clearing came in view. There was Emily, now more seductive to me in sweatshirt and jeans than your standard sexpot in bra and panties. She had her back to me as she greeted Snow White, who approached from the far side of the Clearing, her seven terriers in tow. Emily was fond of Snow White and knelt down to ooh and aah over the Seven Arfs, not even noticing when Mo ran off to romp with S.O.S.

I announced my presence by calling out, "There she is." As Emily turned to see me, I walked right by her. "Good to see you again, Molly. Haven't seen you down here for awhile."

"That's the way it goes at Doglegs," Snow White explained. "It seems like you see the same person five days in a row, then you don't see them for a month."

"Oh, hi Emily," I said, trying my best to make my greeting sound like an afterthought. We smiled knowingly at each other. "Haven't seen *you* around here much lately either."

"Well, I've been kind of ... preoccupied."

"Well, we're glad you're here." With that, I impulsively kissed her on the lips. I was in no mood to keep this romance secret.

"My goodness," Molly observed with some embarrassment. "People are becoming so friendly down here."

"Really? You think so?" I asked, as I literally swept Emily off her feet and cradled her in my arms like a baby. Before setting her down, I planted another kiss on her lips, and Mobile barked at my impertinence. Funny how love can make inhibitions melt away.

"Obviously, you two are beyond friendly."

"Oh, he is *not* acting like a two-year-old, either" said the reverse-talking lady at my side. "What about you, Molly?" she asked, putting on her detective's cap.

"What *about* me?"

"Why isn't there anyone that you're "beyond friendly" with?"

"Oh my, there was a love in my life, but that was a long time ago."

"Did he die?" quizzed the investigator.

"No," said Snow White quietly ... "*it* died."

"Oh, I'm sorry." There was an awkward pause. For a moment, Emily and I weren't sure if "it" referred to love or to a dog. Snow White quickly cleared up the confusion. "Oh, don't be," she responded. "Sometimes love changes." She leaned down to stroke one of her septuplets. "It's part of what makes us human."

"As opposed to canine," I added superfluously. We all smiled.

One of Molly's dogs began to yip uncharacteristically and pulled forward on her leash.

"Trixie must have heard something, or smelled something," said Emily.

"Or maybe it was her sixth sense," added Snow White matter-of-factly. "So I suppose we'll be on our way." She followed her brood in the direction of Webster Field, while Emily and I set out down the second dogleg, heading toward Eden View Park.

"Maybe Trixie's sixth sense told her that I wanted to be alone with you," I offered.

"I don't think that would require a sixth sense. The dog was staring at you when you picked me up and kissed me. Was that really necessary?"

"For Trixie to be staring at me? I don't know. Why don't you ask Trixie?"

Emily laughed. In the first bloom of love, everything's funny. "Well, I can see you've honed your deadpan manner."

"Stick with me fifty years—I'll hone my *bed*pan manner." And, of course, Emily laughed again. How I loved that laugh. And God, were we cute together. We could do no wrong.

Before the second dogleg curves up over a hill to Eden View, there is a fork in the trail. You can take a narrow, weed-covered path that leads into a densely wooded area—it was the route Emily and I had taken during our "getting-to-know-you" session three weeks earlier. Just as we were deciding which path to take, Shep, an aptly named Border collie, came barking and bounding along to make up our minds for us. He herded Mobile and S.O.S. down the secondary path, so Emily and I followed along after them into a more remote part of Doglegs. Shep then started running back to wherever he'd left his owner. But I believe he had other plans for us.

Walking behind Emily, watching the way she moved, a wave passed over me, equal parts happiness and horniness. This was the way all women should move, yet only she had the natural skills to master it, and, apparently, without even trying. Now, all my senses heightened, I swear I picked up the scent of her hair amidst the fresh essence of spring that the light breeze sent streaming toward me. Without any premeditation whatsoever, I grabbed her around the waist from behind and pulled her tightly to me as my lips glommed onto her ear and worked their way down her neck.

She wheeled around toward me, and for one indelible moment, our eyes locked. "What?" she asked, and although there was no mistaking the question, I'm not sure to this day if she actually asked it out loud or with her eyes. Without a word, I reached into my pocket, took out the crumpled paper, and set it firmly in the palm of her hand as both my hands clasped hers.

As she read my hammy but heartfelt declaration, I could see she was focusing so closely on the heartfelt that the hammy totally escaped her. I took her hand and led her off the path to a somewhat secluded glen I had discovered long ago. She didn't ask where we were going or why. She was silent when I took off both of our sweatshirts and laid them out across the bottom of a large hole that S.O.S. and Shela had dug out several weeks earlier. And she didn't say a word when I scooped her up in my arms and gently set her down on the sweatshirts. She understood what was happening as well as I did. Knowing that we were about to do what we were about to do in a place where anybody—or any dog—might find us, put us in awe of our passion. We were, neither one of us, impetuous, risk-taking people by nature. For the moment at least, the strength of our mutual attraction had redefined the meaning of propriety for us, and this new reality was, in itself, highly arousing.

This was not our first time together—just our best. We were at that remarkable place in a relationship where the sex act seemed simultaneously like making meaningful love at the most personal, spiritual level and fucking with the reckless abandon of dogs. Being out there in nature— *with* nature—released all inhibitions in both of us. We did things with each other that morning that we had only dreamed of before. Not only were we making up for our lost week together, we were making up for having being lost from each other our entire lives. I warned you I was a romantic.

Miraculously, we were able to nestle in our little hideaway for nearly an hour without any intruder interrupting the party. Besides our intermittent gasps and moans, the only sounds I remember were the playful snarling and scampering of our dogs. The racket they made seemed to be coming from another galaxy, but they were probably never much more than a few yards away from us. As I pulled on my jeans, I noticed that Mobile had managed to kick up a lot of dirt, creating a mini-hole next to our large one. Apparently, the dogs had taken our rendezvous in stride.

Emily was another matter. She fell uncharacteristically silent, and I sensed she was suddenly embarrassed or having second thoughts about having been a partner in our excellent adventure. I probably didn't help the situation any when, watching her get dressed, I said, "Wait a second," and plucked a maple leaf from her bottom. As I held up the leaf, I expected a laugh. I didn't even get a smile.

Before leaving our makeshift hideaway, Emily sat down and reread my poem. Then she looked up at me. "Matt, I just had a thought. I'm going to put your note where I'll always be able to find it. Right here."

She placed it in the hole and began brushing into it the mounds of dirt encircling its perimeter. Sensing that she was a woman on a mission, I joined her. In no time at all, you'd have never guessed there had ever been a hole there.

"You don't mind, do you Matt?"

"Hell, no. I think it was a great idea. This is hallowed ground."

❋ ❋ ❋

The following weekend, three o'clock or so on a Sunday afternoon, found me—you guessed it—heading down to Doglegs with S.O.S. I swear, the people who lived on my block must have thought I led a very boring life. At any given time, if S.O.S. and I weren't going down the street, we were probably coming up it.

On this particular occasion, I wasn't headed for an encore of the clandestine huddle-'n-cuddle with Emily. She said she was taking Iris to the movies. I was in high spirits nevertheless. It was another beautiful spring day, but very windy. Billowing white clouds rolled swiftly across a picture-book blue sky. S.O.S. hadn't finished his food that morning, pretty unusual for him. I figured I'd let him get a good run in to work up an appetite.

At times the wind grew so gusty it actually whistled, which seemed to spook S.O.S. He barked futilely at something I could not see, and he wasn't in his customary rush to get into the woods. At Webster Field, he went into a hypnotic trance as a couple of kids tried to hoist a kite airborne. When it caught a blast of wind and suddenly shot up and out of his sightline, he snarled in bewilderment. I let him off the leash, and he darted off into the woods.

As I entered Doglegs proper, I met Greg, making the rounds with Hershey and Nestle. He was emptying the poop-filled garbage can that had achieved landmark status at the southernmost point of the woods. Nobody knew how to keep the poop "moving" as well as Greg. After tying up the filled liner bag, he tore a new liner from the sheaf of them that Snow White had donated to Doglegs. He put in the new liner with as much attention to detail as a chambermaid making the bed in the Presidential Suite at the Hilton. I noticed he tied one end of the liner around a handle of the trash can so the liner wouldn't blow away in the wind. He also punctured two holes near the top of the bag, which allowed more air to drain out of it—and more poop to fit into it. Greg had it down to a science.

I knew from personal experience that the filled bags weighed a ton. One time when Greg was sick, I volunteered to deposit a bag in the dumpster behind the elementary school that bordered Doglegs on the northwest. The most efficient way to execute this maneuver was to first heave the bag over the fence that divided Doglegs from the school parking lot. Then you'd climb over the fence and tote the bag to the dumpster. Somewhere along the way, I had managed to throw my back out for a week. But for Greg, it was all in a day's work.

He left the filled bag to pick up on his next pass and decided instead to accompany me down the path. As a veterinarian, I enjoyed talking to Greg because he always had some fresh insights on dogs. A lot of what I learned about them came from books. Greg's wisdom came from extensive firsthand observation. In that department, I have to confess, he had it all over me.

"What's with S.O.S. today? He didn't come up and say hi. In fact, he growled at my boys and trotted right past them."

"Guess he's got other business to attend to."

"Well, whatever it is, I'm sure Nestle and Hershey understand."

This last remark I took at face value. Greg had absolutely no doubt that dogs could tune in to the moods and feelings of other dogs—and of humans—in ways we couldn't understand.

"Remember last fall," Greg continued, "when Nestle had those bladder stones?"

"Do I remember? Who do you think operated on him?"

"Well, we almost brought Hershey in too. When Nestle started whining in pain, Hershey would lay down next to him and start whining too. It wasn't 'til after the operation, when they both returned to normal, that we were sure Hershey had not been whining in agony but in sympathy."

"Lucky for him. Those stones were humungous." We stopped to watch Hershey and Nestle frolicking alongside us. They seemed to confirm that they were now healthy in every way. "Your dogs sure have bonded well ... not just with each other, but with you. They hardly ever seem to leave your sight down here."

"Most dogs—if they're well-treated and healthy and over the age of two—have this natural built-in perimeter, and you're the center point. They won't stray more than a certain distance from you, unless you go after them. But when you move, the perimeter moves too. So I don't go after them. I usually try to keep to the same route, and they always have a pretty good idea of where I am."

"So instead of you finding the dogs, you let the dogs find you."

"Exactly. Once in a while, their noses will get them into trouble. But in the last analysis, they're creatures of—"

Greg never finished his sentence. At that moment, the most chilling scream I had ever heard reverberated through the woods. Whoever would have believed so much meaning could be transmitted by the simple cry, "No!" I sensed it was at once someone's desperate plea for help, their attempt to stop some unspeakable crime in progress, and their refusal to admit the reality of whatever horror they were witnessing.

43

After stopping dead in our tracks and turning to each other for a reality check that confirmed we both heard the same thing, Greg and I charged off toward the north end of the woods. Greg was magnificent in situations like this—once he single-handedly prevented a rapidly spreading fire from potentially leveling Doglegs. Now he was flying through the woods as swiftly as his dogs, and the three of them were soon far ahead of me. If my story had been made into a movie, this is the part where the slow-motion would have kicked in.

I'm not sure of the precise moment my nausea kicked in. It may have started while I was still running and suddenly realizing that I was more intent on finding S.O.S. than the source of the scream. It may have welled up when my progress along the second dogleg suddenly revealed Greg strangling S.O.S. with a huge branch, strategically positioned over my dog's neck in order to pin him to the ground. Or perhaps it began when I knelt down over the hideously mangled body lying next to my dog. A pair of lifeless green eyes stared back at me. The green of those eyes, together with the ribbons of bright red streaming in all directions around them, created a grotesque canvas of color. It conjured up some Christmas gone terribly wrong. As soon as I experienced the shock of recognition, I instinctively turned away. Looking up, I saw Emily standing above me, her face resting in her trembling, bloodied hand.

I held Emily to me for maybe a minute, maybe five. The whole while she was silent, her body hanging limp in my arms. All I could do was whisper over and over into her ear, "I'm so sorry." When I realized how ridiculously inadequate the words sounded, I stopped. There were no tears, not yet. But both of us were shaking.

Greg had immediately called 911 on his cell phone. Then he gathered up Hershey, Nestle, and Mobile and got the hell out of there. As police arrived, Emily pulled away from me. They asked her enough questions to ascertain that she had been out walking with her niece and dog when S.O.S. appeared and began growling. With measured words and a stony face, Emily then explained that her niece knew S.O.S. and approached him with outstretched hand and a, "Whatsa matter, boy?" Then came the attack, unprovoked and unrelenting. Emily screamed, then ran and found a large tree limb lying on the ground. She tried beating the dog off with it and managed to stun him momentarily. Upon recovering, he lunged at Iris again. That's when Greg came up, grabbed the stick from Emily and, with a superhuman effort, broke the dog's neck.

"And do we know the dog's owner?" asked one of the officers.

Emily answered the question by turning toward me. I confirmed it. "S.O.S. is—was—my dog."

The questioning was put on hold as the paramedics arrived. When they covered Iris, Emily began sobbing hysterically. One of the officers told her they had no more questions for her, and she crawled into the back of the ambulance with Iris. I wanted to join her, but the police had more questions for me.

I called out to Emily above the still-howling wind. "I'll meet you at the hospital."

She shook her head so vigorously that the tears streaming down her cheeks began zigging and zagging in all directions. "It's okay, Matt. My sister ... will be there. Don't come tonight." The emphasis placed on the last three words left no doubt that my presence would not be welcome. The ambulance drove off, and the ranking officer began interrogating me.

"Was your dog acting strangely at any time before the attack, Mr. Copeland?"

"No ... as I was walking him down to the park, he seemed a little freaked out by the wind, but there was nothing to suggest ..."

"Rabies?"

"No."

"Has your dog ever exhibited any dangerous behavior prior to this afternoon?"

"Never."

"Ever bitten anyone?"

"Never even snapped at anyone. He was extremely good-natured."

"Do you know—approximately—when your dog had its last rabies shot?"

"Three years ago in December."

"This *past* December?" I nodded. "Mr. Copeland, rabies shots are required for dogs in this state every three years, recommended every two."

"I know that. But in my professional opinion—"

"Your *professional* opinion? ..."

"I'm a veterinarian at the Petacure Clinic in Cameron Heights."

"And you let your own dog go without a rabies shot for over three years?"

"I can explain that. There's a growing body of evidence that dogs and cats are being over-inoculated, and it's resulting in autoimmune disorders and early death. In Georgia they require rabies shots every year. My cousin's down there, and his dog died mysteriously in the prime of life shortly after getting its sixth shot in six years."

"Mr. Copeland, a sixteen-year-old girl is dead, most likely because your dog was *under-inoculated*."

My nausea had been steadily escalating, and I could hold back no longer. I turned around, fell to my knees, and let it all out. Finally, I regained my composure sufficiently to speak. "If my dog had rabies—and I have to admit that seems like the most likely explanation—then I'm guilty of a serious error in judgment."

"Unfortunately, you're also guilty of breaking the law. We have to bring you in." The cops had to do what they had to do. But apparently, my obvious agony and remorse made an impression. "Listen, where do you live?"

"3854 Birchwood. Just up the block."

"We're gonna bring your dog to the lab for an autopsy. You walk home, get yourself cleaned up, and find someone to post bail. It'll probably be $500. We'll pick you up in about an hour."

With ghastly images of Iris and Emily and S.O.S. spinning before my mind's eye, I retraced the route Greg and I had taken through the woods. I tried to think of some positive thought to hold onto. All I could come up with was the fact that the cops had trusted me enough to let me walk home on my own.

Looking up at the darkening sky, I felt trapped under a nightmare. Suddenly I was overcome by an eerily discomfiting sense of unreality. My cognitive functioning told me this was still Doglegs. But my visceral perception put me on some strange, distant planet. Mechanically, I kept putting one leg in front of the other and heading in the direction of what my intellect told me was my home.

At the north end of the woods, I approached the bag of shit that Greg had taken out of the trash can and left sitting alongside the path. I seized on that bag as an opportunity to do something real, something of value. Picking up the bag, I ran over to the fence and hurled it over. Then I hurled myself over. I was in a frenzy to get that bag into the dumpster.

As I lifted up the bag for the final ten yards to the dumpster, the bottom split open and the contents tumbled out. Among the hundred or more Baggies of shit that littered the ground, my eyes focused on the carcasses of two white squirrels that someone—Greg, probably—must have dumped into the trash.

I thought back to that hyper white squirrel I had seen in the park a few weeks ago. Everything was finally becoming numbingly clear to me. My dog hadn't cut himself on broken glass. Why hadn't I connected the dots ... looked for a bite mark on S.O.S.'s paw? I was an idiot. Doglegs was a sham. And the stench—propelled by the strong westerly wind on a perfect trajectory into my face—was overwhelming. After a few dry heaves, I left all the refuse right where it lay and ran home.

※ ※ ※

I spent the night—and all of Monday morning—in a jail cell. If it could happen to me, it could happen to anybody. The sense of unreality that I'd first felt leaving Doglegs persisted. The only thing that seemed real to me was the unreality. All night long, I lay on a cot and stared at the ceiling. I didn't sleep, but not because my mind was overactive. I don't think I consciously thought much about anything that night, certainly not about falling asleep.

On Monday afternoon, the judge set my bail at one thousand dollars. Doug took me home and, to my surprise, I fell asleep immediately and slept through the night. When I woke up, I decided to go in to work. In my desperation, I thought that if I could return to some semblance of my normal routine, maybe I would start to feel normal again. Big mistake.

While I was examining my first—and, as it turned out, last—patient of the day, Dr. Ruskin poked her head in the door and said, "Matt, as soon as you're done here, we have to talk." That translated roughly into, "Matt, as soon as you're done here, you're done here."

When I tell you Dr. Ruskin could have nailed the part of Nurse Ratchet in *Cuckoo's Nest*, you might assume I reached that conclusion based entirely on this final meeting between us. Actually, I had felt that way from day one. Ask Doug. After my initial interview with her, I had described to him how the corners of her mouth turned down when she tried to smile, morphing into a hard-bitten sneer. It was a most unsettling sight. I couldn't help seeing her smile as a reflection of her soullessness. How did I end up working for such a person? How did such a person end up working for dogs? For some questions, there are no easy answers.

My memory of my dismissal is pretty much a blur. In retrospect, it seems like Fate was dictating every action. I don't believe there was any strong reprimand on Dr. Ruskin's part or any real desire to hear my side of the story. Nor was there any concerted effort on my part to save either my job or my dignity. I do remember hearing the terms "negative publicity" and "generous severance." There was also a lot of smiling. Dogs can't smile, and it's to their credit. An involuntary wag of the tail is a much purer response—never duplicitous, never ambiguous.

When she finally said, "Good luck, Matt," she extended her arm to shake my hand. I pretended not to notice, simply said, "Goodbye, Nancy," and walked out of Petacure forever.

I was thankful she had given me the opportunity to make a clean break, not even asking me to stay on for my Tuesday appointments. At that moment, all I wanted to do was see Emily. We hadn't spoken since Sunday. Despite the fact that I had suddenly fallen into an emotional limbo, I somehow knew that reaching some sort of understanding with her was the only hope I had of ever clawing my way back to my former reality.

The funeral, I knew, was a day or two away, and I felt there was a solid chance I would find Emily alone at her apartment now. I needed to confront her head-on. And I purposely didn't call first. I wanted to see what kind of state she would be in when her guard was down, so I decided to take her by surprise.

Instead, she took me by surprise. A spring rain was falling as I ran from the car to her brownstone building. When I arrived in the entryway, I was out of breath and dripping wet. I looked up, and there she was, on the second-floor landing, in a khaki raincoat, on her way out. The first thing that struck me was the sad vulnerability in her eyes and in her bearing. The second thing that struck me was how that sadness gave her a beauty beyond anything even I had ever imagined. And yet she seemed so familiar to me. At that moment, my instinct was to run up and hold her forever, but something held me back. The weariness in her manner communicated a distance greater than the ten steps separating us. I was afraid if I tried to hug her she would break—or we would. She stopped on the landing, frozen like a wax statue. I stood at the foot of the stairs, supplicant to an anguished goddess.

Knowing full well that any words I spoke would be inadequate, I spoke first. "I couldn't call you. I was ... in jail. How are you? How is your family?"

She shrugged and shook her head almost imperceptibly. I plodded on. There was something faintly ridiculous about speaking so emotionally to someone so high above me. An onlooker might have found it humorous. We didn't.

"Can we go inside and talk?"

"My sister is waiting for me."

"Emily, if I had ever thought that Son of Sam could have ..." My voice trailed off.

"Son of Sam? ..." I heard Emily ask softly. "S.O.S. was Son of Sam?" She stared blankly at me—through me.

I stared back in powerless silence. The only sound was the steady patter of the rain. The camel's back was broken, and Emily was walking purposefully down the stairs. As she brushed by me, I grabbed her arm. "Emily, please. I need you to understand ... I made a terrible mistake that I can't undo." My grip tightened. "But I need you to know ... I am not a totally irresponsible person. There's all kinds of disagreement about rabies ... dogs and cats are over-vaccinated ... there's growing evidence."

She glanced down at the hand gripping her sleeve and stiffened. Beneath the vulnerability was a steely strength. She looked me in the eye, and from her cloud of resignation, I saw a flash of anger that ripped through me. "*Dogs and cats*, Matt? Iris is dead. Everything is ... dead."

I let go of her. With those last three words, she had pronounced my sentence and left the courtroom. She drove off in the rain. A moment later, I did too, in the opposite direction.

Suddenly the energy fields surrounding these two men were incompatible, so they could not get close. My master's field reflected nervous uncertainty but passion and excitement. The other's was hollow. I tried to fill the void as best I could. These were two good men but subject to complexities I could not appreciate.

— Shela

Chapter 4
Doug's Turn

No matter how much you love to teach—and I love to teach—one morning a week you wake up, and the first thought that flits across your brain is the same one most students are experiencing: TGIF. But on that first Friday in May, I was especially thankful. The week that was almost over.

I mean, consider my situation. On the home front, my housemate and homey was about ready to put a gun to his head. On the job, the most alive person at school was no longer among the living, and each day one or another of her friends would break down in the middle of third-hour

American History. Of course, the fact that the tragedy at home and the tragedy at school were all part of the same tragedy didn't make matters any easier.

But life goes on. So I'd asked my third-hour students to write an essay about Iris. I thought it would be cathartic for them. And I don't mean to sound flip or callous, but this was a history class, and suddenly Iris was history. I knew she had touched everyone in the class in some way, so I had told each of them to give me one page, double-spaced, on what it was they missed most about her, what they remembered most. I was curious to see what her spirit—still very much alive in her classmates—would inspire.

"OK, who would like to be first to present their recollections of Iris?" No hands went up.

"I know it may be hard to talk about her in front of the class. But afterwards, I have a feeling you'll be glad you did." Still no hands.

"Sheri, you knew Iris pretty well ..."

"Mr. Jesperson, it's too ..."

"It's difficult, I know."

"No ... it's just ... embarrassing. It's going to come off like brown-nosing."

"Brown-nosing? Why?"

"You'll see." Sheri shuffled reluctantly forward, cleared her throat, and began to read. She seemed uneasy at first, but her natural self-confidence soon won out.

"I knew Iris Mohr mostly from history class. I was lucky enough to sit next to her. It didn't take long for me to realize what a special person she was. What I remember most is when she and Mr. Jesperson would get into these big discussions. Even though they seemed to disagree a

lot, you could tell that they both really liked and respected each other. And even though I know Mr. Jesperson tries hard not to play favorites, I think she was his favorite student, and I know he was her favorite teacher.

"Just last week she was so excited because her aunt had taken her to meet a guy she was dating, and it turned out Mr. Jesperson was his roommate. I have to admit, watching the fun the two of them had debating each other in class, I'd feel jealous sometimes.

"But mostly I'd look forward to history just because it was so entertaining. I remember Iris telling him that there was so much killing and torture in the Civil War, she wondered why it wasn't called the Uncivil War. And I'll never forget the day when she tried to make the case that Abraham Lincoln just happened to be in the right place at the right time and was way overrated as a President. That really got Mr. Jesperson going. Sometimes I think she would say things like that just to get him going, because she just enjoyed debating with him so much and also because she liked entertaining the class.

"Other teachers might not know how to handle someone like Iris, but Mr. Jesperson always did. And other kids would be obnoxious if they spoke up in class as much as Iris, but Iris was just cool. Whenever she talked, everyone else would just shut up and listen. And they'd laugh, but never at her, always with her. Iris was just the best."

Sheri went back to her desk, a lot faster than she had left it. Several of the girls in the class were dabbing around the eyes with Kleenex. Only through a supreme effort of the will did I spare myself from joining them.

"Very nice, Sheri, and not just because of the brown-nosing. You know what I think I'm going to do? I'm going to forward some of your essays on to Iris's family. I think it would mean a lot to them."

❋ ❋ ❋

Coming home from school that night took me from the frying pan to the fire. I knew the cloud hanging over my classroom would eventually lift. At home it was more like a nuclear mushroom cloud, and the fallout from that would be contaminating the inhabitants indefinitely.

When I walked in, Matt was lying motionless on the sofa—not asleep, not quite dead, just motionless. Shela was lying on the floor next to the sofa. She stood up and ambled over to me with a gaze that seemed to say, "What are we gonna do about this poor soul?" I rubbed under her collar and spent a moment in silent appreciation for this mainstay of sanity in a world gone mad. Glancing back at the vegetable on the sofa, I realized I was getting tired of tippy-toeing around Matt's fragile emotions. I decided it was time to kick some depressive ass.

"You know, you're wearing a rut in that sofa."

He didn't say boo but, with a courageous effort, managed to assume something resembling a sitting position. He stared up at the ceiling, his head tilted back over a cushion, the rest of him sprawled out with all the vitality of a sack of potatoes.

Finally, he forced out a few words. "How was school today? More tears?"

"Yeah, some ... Matt, you and I used to be able to talk about nothing for hours. Now we've got something that needs to be talked about, and we haven't really talked all week. I'd like to have a clue as to what's going on."

"You know what's going on. You read the papers."

"What's going on in your head, man?" How did you and Emily leave it? Why didn't you go to the funeral?"

"One question at a time, please. Who cares if I didn't go to the funeral? You went. You were my official representative. What was I gonna do, walk up to the Mohrs and say, 'Sorry about my dog killing your daughter? He really didn't mean it, you know. It wasn't S.O.S.'s fault. It was the S.O.B. ... me. My carelessness killed your daughter.'"

"It wasn't carelessness. The newspaper said your professional opinion as a veterinarian was that dogs could go more than three years without a rabies shot."

"Fuck the newspaper. Three years tops. After that, the literature becomes a lot more ambiguous. You want to honestly know why I waited more than three years?"

"You forgot?"

"I wish I could at least say that. You want the honest-to-God truth? Carelessness. Laziness. Self-destructiveness, maybe. The ability to rationalize. The desire to tempt fate. All of the above."

"Goddammit, Matt, you're not self-destructive. You're just human. It was a lapse in judgment. A simple mistake. That's all."

"Right. A simple mistake ... and now I can no longer do the work I love ... or love the woman I love."

"Emily ... she'll come around."

Matt shook his head. "Do you understand what I've done to her? It's over."

"I don't think it's over. And even if it is, you've just gotta say ... what Sinatra would say."

"'Make it one for my baby' ...?"

"No ... 'That's life ... flyin' high in April ... shot down in May' ... but you'll be back on top in June."

Dry of eye and devoid of visible emotion, Matt stood up. "Doug, I appreciate your efforts here. But you know what's the best thing you could do for me right now? Just lemme be."

Right on cue, Shela walked over to the front door and whined. "I guess she hasn't been out since the morning."

"Nope." Matt headed for his bedroom.

"C'mon, girl. You want to go for a walk?!" Her tail started to oscillate like a metronome set to the tempo of *The Sabre Dance*. I'm not sure which one of us was happier to get out of there.

We didn't go to Doglegs. Both Priorwood and Eden View had warned residents to stay out of there until they had a better handle on the rabies threat. So we began walking along the streets that comprised Doglegs' perimeter. Of course, the wisdom of the Doglegs ban was lost on Shela. She kept tugging on her leash in the direction of the park.

But I was too wrapped up in my own internal world to let the tugging bother me. Despite the turmoil raging all around me, I felt I was in a pretty good place just then. As a teacher, I was helping students deal with the pain of losing a popular classmate. As a friend, I was doing my damnedest to talk some sense into Matt.

Any delusions of saintliness I entertained were short-lived. They stopped about the time Shela stopped tugging toward the park and started to pull me straight ahead.

Coming down the block towards us was Mobile, with his owner right behind.

Seeing Emily there suddenly forced me to see myself more sharply, in a light that wasn't altogether flattering. Who was I kidding? I hadn't spent the greater part of these past five days lamenting Iris's death or sharing Matt's grief. I had been fixating on Emily, specifically on the question of how the dynamics of our relationship had changed. Before the catastrophe, I doubt that she'd had much occasion to think of me at all. Afterwards, I was thrust into this paradoxical position. Being Matt's lifelong friend tainted me in her eyes. But being Iris's favorite teacher redeemed me. If nothing else, Emily had to feel powerful ambivalence where I was concerned.

Shela and Mobile weren't handicapped by such complex emotion. Starved for play, they picked up right where they had left off at my house exactly one week earlier. To me, it already seemed like a lifetime away.

Emily eased the tension by speaking first. "Doug, I didn't get to talk to you Tuesday. I want you to know the family appreciated your being there with all of Iris's friends. You know, she always talked about you."

"In a good way, I hope."

"Always in a good way. And that's quite an achievement. Most of her teachers she barely tolerated."

"Well, thank you for telling me. My third-hour class has been ... she's left a gaping hole behind."

"It must be hard for you. You saw her every day ... more often than I did."

"It's been hard for the whole class. I, uh, had them write these essays about her. In fact, they just turned them in today. I've already read them, and some of them really captured her. If you're interested, I could send them on to you. Maybe Iris's parents would—"

"I'd like that, Doug. I'll give you my address."

"That's okay, I can get it from ..." We both knew how the sentence ended. There was an awkward pause.

"Oh dear," Emily said. "We'd better get going." In the process of playing with Shela, Mobile had wrapped his leash around Emily so that neither one of them could move. With some difficulty, we managed to unwind the chain. Then Emily and Mo continued on their way. Shela and I watched as they marched off.

If I was going to play this game with any hope of success, I would have to take it slow and play it smart.

Life can be delicious. Even before he scratched my ears, I sensed this one would taste good. Reflexively, my tongue poured out, and the tip curled as my taste buds positioned themselves for the dunking. They were not disappointed. Epidermal secretions reflect the quality of the person. This guy was quality. I went back for seconds.

— Bubba

Chapter 5
Matt's Turn

For what I was experiencing in the ensuing weeks and months, I discovered there was a medical term—a psychiatric term. Derealization, they call it. Not nearly as publicized as depression or anxiety, it incorporates elements of both. The overriding feeling is a detachment from reality caused by an inability of the nervous system to process all the incoming stimuli in a normal way. Enough of the brain still functions properly so, intellectually, you're aware that what appears unreal is actually real. But viscerally you're walking around in a nightmare. You can converse with people normally enough that your misery may escape their notice entirely, but all the while you're thinking that they hold the key to a kingdom of unimaginable bliss. And not only can you not find the key—you don't even see the door.

When I told my primary physician what was going on in my life, he didn't hesitate to prescribe Prozac. But he warned me it wouldn't start to kick in for awhile.

Prozac or no Prozac, if my circuits were overloaded, there was no relief in sight. Two court cases were pending. The state had charged me with involuntary manslaughter, the Mohrs with wrongful death. Until these cases were settled—and in my favor—my career was as dead as my dog.

At the time, I could count no blessings. In retrospect, there were two. One was my Uncle Don. He was an attorney and convinced there was enough empirical evidence to make a case for less frequent rabies shots. With that evidence, he assured me, the court would mitigate my sentence. He didn't ask me any more questions than he had to, and I didn't ask him any questions, period. It was all too overwhelming for me.

I preferred to spend my time with my second blessing, Shela. When Doug's school year ended in June, he went right into summer school, so Shela and I spent a lot of time alone together. Alone, but rarely lonely. We'd take long walks through Doglegs in the late morning or early afternoon, when I could usually avoid encountering all the regulars, with their judgmental stares or morbid curiosity. Not once did I encounter Emily.

Of course, even during "rush hour," Doglegs was not what it used to be. Overnight, the place had undergone massive change. I now tended to divide my existence into

B.C. (Before Carnage) or A. D. (After Debacle). B.C., Doglegs' patrons all had an Ozzie-and-Harriet aura about them. A.D., Ozzie and Harriet had given way to George and Martha, and not just through my distorted lens. The quakes that had rocked my world created a schism that reached into everyone else's. Paranoia reigned supreme. Suddenly people were finding all sorts of excuses not to make the trip to Doglegs. And those who did hardly ever seemed to have much time to stop for a friendly word. After all, behind most any bush could lurk a rabid squirrel or a killer dog.

Or a bloodthirsty lawyer. B.C., Ben Schallert and I had always stopped to chitchat. These days he was no doubt stopping to chitchat with other Dog People *about* me. On the one awkward occasion when our paths crossed in June, Ben simply smiled—or was it a smirk?—and kept walking.

He had plenty to smirk about. Early in June, Woodman had come barreling down the main path toward the Clearing armed with an eight-foot-long tree limb. It struck Marie, owner of Shep the Border collie, just below the knee. That might not have posed a problem had not the force of the blow sent Marie tumbling into the ditch—Shela's ditch—at the Clearing. Fortunately for Doug, Marie did not know Shela was prime mover of the dirt that had once filled that hole. What Marie did know is that she now had a broken vertebra and Elaine, Woodman's owner, was going to pay for it in court. This incident, coming right on the heels of the much greater tragedy, had sent Doglegs reeling from a devastating one-two punch.

In both cases, Ben was a key player. He was representing Marie in the Woodman incident. Through his acquaintance with Emily, he also got the nod to prepare the wrongful death case against me for Iris Mohr's parents. For his visits to Doglegs with Justice these days, Ben stuffed business cards into his pockets as religiously as doggie bags. Evidently, he had them specially printed for the Dog People. Greg had shown me one of them. It featured a picture of him with his dog. Underneath, a caption read, "Justice and Justice's lawyer." Heaven help us all.

Ben was about the only one pleased with the turn of events. Sullen expressions and hurried steps were now the norm in the woods. But these weren't the only visible evidence of Doglegs' demise. The tree-lined paths had become shit-lined as well. Apparently, no one now saw the logic in cleaning up after their dogs. And as the shitpiles multiplied, so did the flies. Greg had no intention of cleaning up the mess, and who could blame him?

Not me, certainly. Greg had treated me the same after the attack as before it. I was grateful to those people who hadn't made a pariah of me. I could count them on the fingers of one hand.

Snow White was another member of that select group. She made her daily pilgrimage to Doglegs as always, and even in my despondent state—or perhaps because of it—I knew that at some level I was glad to see her. One particular meeting stands out in my mind. It was shortly after the Fourth of July holiday. She and I were the only ones at the Clearing, so one-on-one rules were in effect. In other words, we would have the opportunity to go beyond the superficial pleasantries that until recently had been part and parcel of Doglegs' social ethic.

"Good morning, Matt. Hi there, Shela."

"Morning, Molly. And how are the Seven Wonders of the World today?"

"Only six now, Matt, unless you're counting me."

I took a quick head count and saw that there were indeed only six Yorkies present. "Where's ..."

"Chester. We lost him over the Fourth. It was the noise of the fireworks. That always did get him worked up into a frenzy. This year, I think it was just a little more than his old heart could take."

"It must be hard for you."

"Not so bad."

"Really?"

"You know, Matt, people think I'm a saint to keep so many dogs. You want to know why I really do it? Truth is, I'm a selfish old biddy, looking out for old number one. So I spread the love around. That way, when one of them dies, you just lose a little piece of your heart, not the whole darn thing."

"I think you're onto something there, Molly. Losing S.O.S. was ... it was—" I cut myself off before I started feeling too much. But Snow White continued for me.

"Sure, it was tough. But you lost a lot more than S.O.S., didn't you?" I sort of nodded, warily, letting her know that, although I wasn't entirely comfortable with where she was heading, I had no intention of stopping her. Between the two of us, whatever happened in Doglegs was fair game.

Bending over, she let all six of her dogs off the leash. She did it so quickly, so deftly, I almost thought there was some sleight-of-hand involved. Then, without missing a beat, she picked up her train of thought.

"Losing a person you love ... it's tougher than losing a dog."

"Even for a dog person?"

"Even a dog person is still a person."

"Maybe it would have been easier if I'd done what you did."

"Somehow I can't see you with seven dogs, Matt."

"No, I mean, if I'd had seven girlfriends. You know, spread the love around."

Molly laughed heartily. Then she turned serious again. "The thing about dogs is, you've only got about ten years with them, fifteen if you're lucky. You know it going in. You know it, and they know it too."

"*They* know it?" Now I was the one who was laughing.

But Snow White wasn't. "Of course they know it. Why do you think they have this uncanny ability to make every minute count? When they play, they play hard. When they rest, they go into this hibernation-like trance that's nirvana to them. God only knows what they're thinking then. But when they die, they have no regrets."

I glanced about and saw her Yorkies, all very engrossed, sniffing trees, peeing on bushes, jumping on one another. Their liveliness at that moment seemed quite unusual for them and—in the context of Molly's theorizing—almost poignant.

"And you're telling me this now because? ..."

"Part of the reason dogs form such loyal bonds to us is they know we're going to be with them for their entire life. On the other hand, *we* know they probably won't be there for *our* entire life, so we try not to let our feelings for them get too intense. But when you fall in love with a person, Matt, you're programmed to hope it's going to be for life. So you invest the object of your affection with all kinds of superhuman qualities. *Super*human, not human. None of us can possibly live up to that. That's why it's so difficult for two human beings to maintain a dog-like devotion to each other. Our lives go on too long, and we complicate them much too much. People are just ... unpredictable."

"So, basically, what you're saying is, if we want to play it smart, we'll stick with dogs."

"Not necessarily, Matt. If we want to play it *safe*, we'll stick with dogs." With that, she smacked her lips together a few times, emitting sounds that were a cross between kisses and bird calls. Immediately, her contingent all came trotting over to her. She had those dogs back on leash almost as quickly as she had let them off. The dexterity of her hands matched the agility of her mind.

As she began her walk back home, she called over her shoulder. "Keep your eye on the big picture, Matt. It's bigger than you think." Though I didn't know exactly what she meant, I was convinced that *she* did. And I couldn't help but notice that the world that had seemed such a hopeless jumble to me before our conversation had for the moment become a dangerous, exciting jumble. A fine distinction, perhaps, but one that seemed to make a world of difference as I continued down the path. I don't know, maybe it was just the Prozac finally kicking in.

Somewhere along the second dogleg, a lady named Cheryl approached. We'd had some cordial chats in the past, but this time she simply gave me a forced, "Hi," and kept on walking at a measured paced. Bubba, her gangly black-and-tan, came bounding up the path behind her.

67

He'd always reminded me of S.O.S. A big goofball with a heart of gold. Apparently, no one had apprised Bubba of Doglegs' new code of conduct. He jumped up and planted a big wet kiss on my lips.

Down the path, Cheryl began calling, "Bubba ... c'mon boy." But Bubba was in no hurry. I had instinctively knelt down to scratch the dog's ears, and he began licking my face like it was a liver-flavored lollipop. Some dogs chased balls. Some chased squirrels. Some were diggers. Some were wrestlers. Bubba, more than anything, was a licker.

Cheryl kept calling. As her voice became more insistent, it also became fainter. Clearly, she had made up her mind she was not going to come back and suffer the unpleasantness of having to make small talk with me. She was counting on Bubba to eventually come to his senses.

But Bubba just kept on licking, and I did nothing to discourage it. Maybe he simply was responding to the salt in my sweat on that hot July afternoon, but in my affection-starved state, it felt like a sweet combination of love and sympathy.

Finally, Cheryl did have to subject herself to the embarrassment of coming back, leashing him, and hauling him away. She didn't give me so much as a word or a glance. Cheryl used her lack of communication to communicate her disapproval at my being a party to Bubba's little mutiny. Without remorse, I simply smiled.

When they were out of sight, I found myself sitting on a tree stump. Bubba's licking unleashed a wave of memory and emotion that momentarily filled the hole in my heart. Everything that S.O.S. had taken with him now became intensely palpable. The bond between us once again seemed very much alive, so how could it be that he was not?

For the first time A.D., I wept. I wept for what S.O.S. had given me, and for what he had taken away. I wept for how inconceivable it all was to him, and for how inconceivable it all was for me. I wept for Emily, for Iris, and for the intermingled joy and pain of life. And when the tears finally stopped, I almost felt a part of the planet again.

I still didn't have the key. But at least I could see the door.

As a creature of habit, I'd been lucky. My mistress had always acted predictably—in fact, she hadn't acted at all. She was as natural as one of us. But now her voice takes on a subtly higher pitch that is just not her. Her smiles are forced, her laughter fabricated. It's enough to make any dog uneasy when the gods stumble.

— Mobile

Chapter 6
Emily's Turn

The funeral was a blur. For the four preceding days and nights, I had been pummeled by one painful emotion after another. First came the shock and grief. Then the guilt that I'd been pushing aside from the beginning moved front and center, helped along by the accusing gazes of my sisters.

As for the blame their silent stares showered upon me, I couldn't be sure how much was real and how much I imagined. All that mattered was that I started to believe my role in the tragedy fully justified their disdain. Hadn't I always been the one who encouraged Iris's fascination with all things canine? Throughout her fateful, final visit to Doglegs, wasn't I the one who was with her—and obviously not with her closely enough? Most damning of all, hadn't I brought this murderous animal into her life through my ill-conceived liaison with a man who flagrantly breached veterinary ethics?

Yes. Yes. Yes. In my unhinged condition, I pronounced myself guilty on all counts. And living with the verdict—God, it *wasn't* hard! Guilt quickly gave way to rage. All the misery reduced itself to one simple truth: Matt had betrayed me. He had taken Iris out of my life, and, in the process, effectively removed himself as well. This was a man I thought would move heaven and hell for me. Instead, he simply moved me from one to the other.

The brain, the mind, the nervous system, whatever, can take only so much. By the time the funeral rolled around on Wednesday, I was basically numb. One thing I do remember is that Doug shepherded about a dozen students—Iris's friends and classmates—who marched up to the front row to pay their respects to us before the service. Each of the students carried an iris and solemnly handed it to Melissa, Iris's mother, so that she held a full bouquet by the time their procession was over.

Doug followed the students. He stopped in front of me, looked sadly into my eyes, took my hand, and planted a light condolence kiss on my cheek. Something about it gave me a vague impression that he wasn't simply acting as delivery boy for Matt. This was no peck by proxy. It originated with Doug, out of his feelings for my niece and myself.

At the cemetery, Melissa spontaneously adorned the casket with her iris bouquet, to be buried with its namesake.

This gesture prompted several of Iris's friends to glance glowingly in Doug's direction, making it clear to me that he was the one who had conceived and orchestrated the presentation of the flowers.

Sitting in the living room late that night with my sisters, I learned Doug had made a positive impression. "I don't care if he *is* your friend's roommate. I like him," offered Carrie, my middle sister. Even Melissa, who had hardly spoken a word all night, nodded agreement.

No one would mention Matt by name. They simply referred to him as "your friend." "He's not my friend anymore," I said.

Carrie was doing her best to get a conversation going, no easy task given the condition of her two sisters. "I actually think Doug's the nicer-looking of the two."

My overriding wish at that moment was to be home with Mobile. In the weeks that followed, my non-judgmental companion was my sole source of support. His big, brown spaniel eyes radiated a softness that said, "Hang in there. Everything will be okay." Far from tainting my canine connection, S.O.S.' monstrous act drew me closer to Mobile. Matt's negligence helped me appreciate how dependent dogs are on the actions of humans. That realization served to fuel my outrage. I resolved to shut Matt out of my life. To my mind, he was beyond redemption.

Doug was another matter. A week or so after the funeral, he sent me some essays his students had written about Iris. One of those essays described the mutual admiration society of Doug and Iris. When I discovered that Iris had

had a genuine kinship with Doug, I guess I began to feel a kinship with him as well.

All through July, I could not yet bring myself to venture into the woods. Most of the Dog People shared my aversion. Mo and I would run into Doug and Shela at various points around Doglegs' perimeter. Sometimes we'd let the dogs romp together unleashed in Eden View Park. Doug was always friendly, but in a respectful kind of way, careful to keep his emotional distance. I found myself curious to know him better.

One hot Sunday afternoon in August, I got the opportunity. As I pulled up in front of my apartment on the way back from grocery shopping, there he was, with Shela, waving to me from the sidewalk.

"We've got to stop meeting like this," I joked, as I took my bags out of the car.

"What do you mean? We've never met like this."

"What do *you* mean?" I laughed. And my laugh kind of startled me. I don't think I'd so much as chuckled in three months.

"Well, anytime I ever bump into you, Mo is by your side. Today you're traveling solo. Is Mobile immobilized or something?"

"Hey, the air conditioning in my car is *not* broken. And my car is *not* hot, Doug. He would have suffocated in there today."

"Tell me about it. Look at Shela's tongue." I looked. It was hanging almost down to the sidewalk, and she was panting heavily.

"Say, if you think she can make it up a flight of stairs, she can have a drink out of Mo's water dish."

Just then we heard Mo barking. Doug looked up and saw him at the second-floor window. "Apparently, Mo has some other ideas."

I managed to muster up some mock-indignation. "Mo is not that kind of dog. I didn't raise him to keep all the water for himself."

"Then we've got a deal. I'll even carry up one of your bags."

Ten minutes later we were sitting at the kitchen table, nursing soft drinks and watching our dogs' interaction, or lack of it. Shela sniffed around Mo a bit, trying to get some reaction out of him. But Mo was settled comfortably in a corner, content to mung on the remnants of an old rawhide bone.

There was a pause in the conversation. Doug absent-mindedly shook the ice around in his glass.

"Emily, ya know ... I ... uh ... appreciate this hospitality. I know our friendship is a little awkward because of ... the circumstances."

"Because of Matt, you mean." Doug nodded, and I summoned up my most nonchalant manner. "Say, how is Matt anyway?"

"Better. Better than he was. But kind of in a state of limbo with trial number one coming up in a couple of weeks."

At the mere mention of the trial, I could feel my body tensing up, and a cloud moving over our table. I had never been vindictive by nature, but I was hellbent on the notion that Matt was going to pay an appropriate price for a heinous crime. And it was more than a matter of simple justice. By being my family's most vocal crusader for his conviction, I believed that I might remove any doubt as to where my sympathies lay, redeem myself in the eyes of my sisters, and honor the memory of my niece. I had convinced myself that taking a strong stand to secure Matt's guilt would somehow expiate my own.

Doug sensed my discomfort. "Sorry to bring that up. We probably shouldn't be discussing it."

"Hey, it's on your mind. The defendant is your best friend, and the victim was ..."

" ... my best student."

"Puts you in an awkward position, doesn't it, Doug?"

"No more so than you."

"How am I in an awkward position? Matt and I are history."

"Yeah, that's what he says too. But can you really just make a clean break like that?"

I shook my head slowly, and Doug must have noticed that my eyes were staring at something far removed from my apartment. "Every time I think of him, I see Iris lying there. I can't help it, Doug. That's just the way it is."

"Well, for what it's worth, I think the judge and jury are going to see it your way."

"You think so? I know Matt has got this argument about poor, over-inoculated dogs. Even our own lawyer told us there's no proven case of a dog becoming rabid when they've had a shot within the last six years."

"Listen, Emily." Doug paused. I sensed he was mulling over what he was about to say—or whether he was actually going to say it. "Matt told me he knew that after three years the risk could begin to grow. He admitted that he was irresponsible—he basically said he just never took the time to do what he knew he should do. It's as simple as that."

I stopped to take in the significance of Doug's bombshell. Pivotal evidence had fallen right in my lap. All of a sudden I knew how Bob Woodward must have felt when he scored Deep Throat.

"Doug, I've got to ask ... Would you ...?"

" ... tell it to the judge? Yeah. I would. I will."

"You'd go against Matt for my sake?"

"Not for your sake. For the sake of justice ... just like you're doing."

"Doug, I—"

"If I'm asked to be a witness for the prosecution, I will tell the truth. End of discussion."

As it turned out, it *was* the end of the discussion, because at that moment Mo began gagging, an all-too-familiar warning that preceded his vomiting as surely as lightning precedes thunder. The four of us all bounded down the stairs, and Mo bolted out the door and into the brownstone's bushes just in time to noisily heave forth pieces of rawhide in a mysterious puddle best left undescribed.

When we got him back in the vestibule, Doug leashed Shela and thanked me again. He pressed his lips to my forehead. Impulsively, I kissed him on the cheek. What we had in common was that Iris had captivated us both. The spark she had shared with each of us separately now seemed to kindle something that glowed warmly when we were together.

Doug turned back and smiled as he walked out the door. "Shela says, 'Thanks for the water.'"

"Anytime."

Some say I'm pushy, but it's for their own good. I am a mover. The satisfaction of getting everyone where they need to be is what drives me. No dog will be content at the living-room window once they've experienced Doglegs. And if I could herd the humans back there, I would. I'd round them up into one big clump and force them to stick together.

— Shep

Chapter 7
Matt's Turn

It started sometime in August, just before my trial. Bubba, I believe, was first to break ranks. Cheryl had opened her front door to take a package from the mail carrier when the mutinous mongrel brazenly made his getaway.

The very next day, Boomer, a big Dalmatian full of piss and vinegar, literally went over the fence. Shela and Mo took a different route, digging their way under their fences.

Marie Olsen—Shep the Border collie's owner—told the most bizarre tale. Early one evening, Ben Schallert had stopped to talk to her as they walked their dogs down my street. When they approached Webster Field, the dogs began jerking forward with such force that both Ben and Marie dropped their leashes. If Marie is to be believed—and I have no reason to doubt her—Shep then grabbed the handle of Justice's leash in her mouth and, with Justice in tow, flew off to the woods like a wide receiver, pigskin in hand, flies off to the end zone. Talk about taking the herding instinct to the next level!

Though the means of escape varied, the destination was invariably Doglegs' woods. Greg told me that on any given day, at any given time, he'd see half a dozen dogs roaming around with nary an owner in sight.

For the first few weeks, the owners would come into the woods and coax their pets home with dog treats and outstretched arms. But eventually—after the cities of Priorwood and Eden View issued a joint statement declaring the suburbs rabies-free—a growing consensus formed among the Dog People. The thinking went something like this: *Our dogs miss Doglegs, but we don't. So if they want to go down there by themselves, we'll let them stay. When they get hungry or lonesome, they'll come home.*

And that's what happened. In fact, by mid-September the Dog People were routinely opening doors and gates so that their Rovers could come and go at will. Sometimes they'd disappear for days at a time. Even the local police and the Parks Department looked the other way. As long as the dogs were otherwise well-behaved and sticking closely to the woods, nobody seemed to mind.

I know what you're thinking. Dogs are not capable of staging a mass walkout, or runout—let alone a successful one. But how else do you explain the phenomenon that cut a swath through our Priorwood-Eden View community?

Personally, I like to think it was more than a case of dogs pining for Doglegs. I believe they missed the B.C. life *in toto*, when everybody—two-leggers and four-leggers—just got along. According to my theory, the dogs came to the woods in hopes of drawing their owners there. At some level, I think the canines sensed that, with everyone back at Doglegs again, we could begin to break down the barriers that now separated us. The dogs wanted the Dog People to become a real people again.

That's what I think. Of course, you already know what a lunatic I am.

※ ※ ※

On a Saturday afternoon in the waning days of summer, I returned home from a final strategy meeting with my Uncle Don. The trial was just a few days away. Uncle Don, God bless him, had just given me a pep talk that would have done Knute Rockne proud. He was on a righteous crusade to clear my name. Apparently, he envisioned that my acquittal would be his last hurrah—the crowning achievement of a less-than-remarkable legal career.

Together we had sifted through reams of research in pursuit of reliable guideposts for the frequency of canine rabies vaccinations. Vets who still gave annual shots acted mainly on the basis of tradition rather than scientific evidence. Even those who scheduled shots every two or three years did so to comply with state or local ordinances, not as a result of direct evidence that a dog could become rabid if the vaccination interval increased. But nobody could say for sure that a rabies shot would remain effective after three years.

Evidence that frequent vaccination jeopardized canine health was equally elusive. Some biochemists speculated that the buildup of antibodies resulting from frequent vaccination could trigger autoimmune diseases like lupus, where a dog's antibodies attack its own cells instead of invading viruses. But the only meaningful hard data we found applied to cats, which showed increased risk of developing sarcomas at the point of injection.

I already had a passing familiarity with most of the information from reading professional journals and online bulletins. Despite the lack of compelling evidence, Uncle Don told me he had enough to paint a persuasive portrait of a veterinarian who had made a personal choice not to vaccinate his dog based on his honest assessment that it was in the best interests of the dog and posed virtually no threat to the community. My uncle admitted there was little chance of having my veterinary license reinstated in the foreseeable future. But he did seem confident I would escape the manslaughter conviction the prosecution was after. Then I could get on with my life, such as it was.

Uncle Don's most recent counsel had helped me fend off my funk a bit, but it returned with a vengeance after I got home. What had been gnawing at me all along was the fact that I wasn't wholly convinced of my own defense. First of all, I should have recognized before the attack that S.O.S.'s strange behavior was consistent with symptoms of rabies. But even more incriminating, who was I to have gambled on the limits of how long a dog could go without a rabies shot? This wasn't Vegas. The stakes were much higher. Whether I was guilty of hubris or stupidity, I couldn't be sure. But of my guilt I had no doubt.

The house was dark and quiet. Shela, my constant companion of late, had run off to Doglegs early that morning and not yet returned. Doug had said he was going to spend most of the afternoon at school to prepare something-or-other for his class. My aloneness quickly ripened into loneliness.

I have to say, I missed Shela a lot more than I did Doug. Lately he'd been out a lot, but even when he was there, it seemed like he wasn't. He'd become so reticent and remote, you'd think *he* was the one about to go on trial for murder. Throughout the summer, I had found his lack of support a surprise and a disappointment. But I never said word one to him about it. Giving him the benefit of the doubt, I interpreted his emotional distance as the normal reaction of a friend who was deeply affected by the tragedy, commiserating with me deeply on the inside, but simply at a loss as to what to say or do.

Reclining on the La-Z-Boy in the living room, I soon fell into my A.D. activity of choice—wallowing in thoughts of Emily. We hadn't spoken or seen each other since that rainy May morning in her brownstone entryway. But she was all around me. Her mere existence sustained me like a sun hidden behind a cloud.

To break the silence, I turned on the radio. Rod Stewart was singing ...

A cigarette that bears a lipstick's traces
An airline ticket to romantic places
And still my heart has wings
These foolish things remind me of you ...

The song lifted me up because he didn't sing it in the traditional way. Instead of a mournful lament, it was joyous and hopeful. They'd get back together, or, if they didn't, the memory of her would suffice ...

How strange, how sweet, to find you still
These things are dear to me
They seem to bring you so near to me ...

As the upbeat arrangement sucked me in, the sickeningly sweet optimist locked somewhere deep inside of me was threatening to break through. What I wanted more than anything was to go to her, simply for the selfish pleasure of seeing those eyes and hearing that voice again. But I couldn't go just to say how much I loved her or how sorry I was. I had to tell her something she didn't already know. Something major. Unfortunately, I wasn't pregnant with her child.

Then it hit me. One solution that would solve two dilemmas. I would plead guilty at my trial. That would ease the demons that taunted me. More immediately, it would furnish an excuse to see Emily. She would be the first to hear this newsworthy nugget. I would tell her of my decision and come up with some eloquent way to explain how I had reached it. Uncle Don might disown me, but who knows what Emily might do? Considering the potential rewards, a little jail time and my uncle's scorn seemed a small price to pay.

I turned off the radio, splashed some cold water on my face, combed my hair. Before I had time to second-guess myself, I was pulling up at Emily's apartment, climbing her stairs, rapping on her door. Mo had been barking from the moment I entered the building.

Silently, I counted the seconds until Emily came to the door. Maybe I did it to assure myself it was not an eternity that was passing. After about eight seconds—and 800 heartbeats—the door opened.

Doug and I simply stared at each other. I guess that's when I should have started counting the seconds, because I have no idea how long we stood there like that. For a moment, I could comprehend the power of the canine sense of smell. Emily's scent was all over him. I briefly toyed with the notion of throwing a sucker punch. That wasn't my style.

When Doug had first opened the door, Emily was sprawled out on her sofa. Obviously, my unexpected appearance disconcerted her. From the corner of my eye, I saw her jump quickly to her feet and brush her tousled hair back from her eyes. I made a conscious effort not to look directly at her. Feeling like Perseus confronting the Gorgon Medusa, I was afraid that seeing her under these circumstances would suck the lifeblood out of me. No way was I about to let a little thing like reality tarnish my idealized perception. So I was left with the lame choice of eyeballing Doug, staring into space, or focusing on Mobile.

Mobile made sure it was no contest. Thanks to him, this surreal encounter quickly went from the ridiculous to the sublimely ridiculous. Unlike the rest of us, Mo was not taken aback in the least. At first, he simply jumped up on me. When I absent-mindedly began scratching the back of his neck, his forelegs locked around my calf. He began to hump me with abandon, seemingly oblivious to the human dynamic taking place. His shamelessness fit the proceedings about as well as a fart at a funeral.

The dichotomy between his apparent innocence and our lack of it turned a serious confrontation into a seriocomic one. I felt Emily and Doug had to be on the verge of giggles, because I was. While Mo may have been doing his utmost to diffuse a delicate situation, I intended to leave with at least a shred of dignity—and pant leg. Without a word from anyone, I managed to free my leg and flee the apartment. No one tried to dissuade me.

❋ ❋ ❋

When I got home, I went straight to my closet, took out my suitcase, and packed. For the duration of the trial, I'd stay with someone who was still in my corner—Aunt Maura and Uncle Don.

On my way out the door, I saw Shela come prancing up the walk. Actually, I think I smelled her before I saw her. Even for an experienced dog sniffer like myself, the stench was incredibly foul.

"What have you been rolling around in girl, huh?"

She didn't have to answer. I could see wads of shit clinging to both of her flanks. But there was also an essence of dead skunk about her. Apparently, she had taken advantage of everything Doglegs had to offer.

Without hesitating, I brought her into the house and led her to Doug's bedroom. Invitingly, I patted his unmade bed and laid a fresh rawhide bone on the pillow. "C'mon, Shela, I think you're ready for a nice, long nap." She hopped right up and settled in with the bone.

My work was done there, and I headed to my aunt-and-uncle's. Now I was full of fight, and Uncle Don's defense seemed airtight. The only difference was, we'd no longer be able to use Doug as a character witness. I was now fairly certain that would be an uncomfortable role for him.

More to the point, I no longer knew who Doug was. Having feelings for his best bud's girl—that's been done to death, and I could live with that. But acting on those feelings was a serious breach of friendship. And acting behind my back—and right under my nose—made it an irreparable breach. I didn't think he had it in him. Something had changed him. Knowing that this something was Emily, made his betrayal at once comprehensible and incomprehensible to me.

As for Emily's willingness to be a party to this madness, the explanation eluded me. I sifted through the possibilities, trying to give both her and myself the benefit of the doubt. Doug was a lot like me—everybody said so—and she just wanted to replace me with a version of me that hadn't committed my transgression. Or, she was just trying to hurt me, and you always hurt the one you love. Or, Iris held a special place in both of their lives, and her relationship with Doug simply helped Emily heal the trauma of her niece's death.

Two days into the trial, another explanation presented itself. Doug took the oath, took the stand, and took the wind out of my sails. Uncle Don and I sat there and put on our best poker faces as the holier-than-thou prosecutor questioned his star witness.

"Mr. Jesperson, what was your relationship to Iris Mohr?"

"I was her history teacher at Kennedy High in Eden View."

"And she was a good student?"

"Iris was the best."

Uncle Don stood up. "Objection, Your Honor. The victim's academic record is immaterial to this case."

The District Attorney countered, "Your Honor, prosecution simply seeks to establish the admiration the witness had for the victim since we believe it may have a bearing on the credibility of the witness's testimony."

"Overruled."

The D.A. nonetheless decided not to pursue the Doug/Iris Mutual Admiration Society line of questioning and cut to the chase.

"Mr. Jesperson, please tell the court how you know the defendant."

"We were best friends since the third grade."

"You say you *were* best friends? You're no longer best friends?"

Doug hesitated. "Well, after my testimony today ..."

"Mr. Jesperson, prior to the events of April 27, had you ever had a discussion with the defendant on the subject of rabies?"

"Yes, we had."

"And what was the nature of that discussion?"

"Well, one day I was playing with S.O.S., and I happened to look at his rabies vaccination tag. I noticed the year engraved on there was 2004."

"2004. And when was it you noticed that?"

"Early this year."

"2008?"

"Right."

"And what was your reaction?"

"I just said, 'Hey, Matt, did you forget to put a new rabies tag on Son of Sam?'"

"Son of Sam?"

With a sheepish half-smile, Doug explained. "Oh, yeah, that was S.O.S.'s actual name."

Doug acted embarrassed, as though he had accidentally let some information slip out that he'd have preferred to keep secret. As I tried to grapple with what I was hearing, I felt a faint wave of nausea well up from the pit of my stomach. Nausea triggered by B.S.

Uncle Don, God love him, raised another objection, and this time it was sustained. The judge ruled the dog's name was irrelevant to the case. But my guess was that the jury thought otherwise. The damage had been done.

Without missing a beat, the D.A. continued. "And when you asked about the rabies tag, what was the defendant's response?"

"He said S.O.S. hadn't had a rabies shot since 2004."

"And how did you reply to that?"

"Well, I told him that Shela—my dog—gets one every two years."

"And what was his reaction?"

"Oh, he said something like, 'Hey, who's the vet here, you or me?' He just kind of shrugged it off."

I squirmed in my seat. My memory was as good as his. He was simply being truthful now. And I knew what was coming next.

The D.A. paused and looked thoughtful, as if he didn't know what was coming next, as if he hadn't choreographed every last shred of testimony. "What about *after* April 27? Were there any further conversations with your roommate about the vaccination issue?"

"I remember one."

"Tell us about it."

"Well, it was about a week after. Matt was pretty depressed, and I was trying to cheer him up. I told him he must have had some solid medical evidence for waiting as long as long as he did to revaccinate his dog."

"Go on ..."

"He basically said the medical literature was pretty inconclusive. He ... was beating himself up. He said he was just lazy ... careless ... he knew S.O.S. should have had the shot after three years tops."

"You could say he felt guilty?"

"You could say that, yes."

"No further questions, Your Honor."

❋ ❋ ❋

I can't say I was surprised by what transpired. The surprise was my reaction to it. I'd had a strong suspicion Doug was going to desert me. But watching that desertion play out in the courtroom reduced me to a seething, trembling bundle of nerves. The realization that he had simply told the truth only served to deepen my fury and throw me into a state of confusion. Doug had let me down. Worse than that, *I* had let me down. No one could be trusted, not even your own self. Who the hell was I, anyway? The bedrock I had built my identity on seemed to be shifting under me.

With my footing in jeopardy, I nonetheless managed to walk out of the courtroom at recess. That's when my eyes happened to focus for one terrible moment on a brazen spectacle that immediately etched itself into the deepest recesses of my brain. Amidst the throng in the antechamber, I saw in profile a man and a woman standing, facing one another, inches apart, gazing fondly into each other's eyes. He held both of her hands tenderly in his. They were blissfully unaware of my presence, oblivious to everyone and everything else in that room. In retrospect, they were probably just exchanging pleasantries. But for the effect that scene had on me, they may as well have been exchanging bodily fluids. Truth may have informed Doug's testimony, but Beauty inspired it.

As I watched them, Emily and Doug happened to turn so that their backs were toward me. He cupped his arm lightly around her back and waist. At that very moment, I felt a hand on my shoulder, and I jumped.

"Settle, boy."

"You startled me, uncle." Don looked concerned, so I tried to be glib. "I wish I *could* settle—out of court." He still looked concerned.

With his hand clasped onto my shoulder—for physical guidance as much as moral support—he led me over to a nearby, empty office. We sat down, and I knew it was time for Uncle Don's favorite pastime: going over our strategy. He was earnest, and he was upbeat. I'll give him that.

But his Pollyanna posturing was so far removed from my anesthetized mental state that his words seemed to be coming at me from the end of a very long tunnel. I saw no light beyond them.

Before I took the stand, Uncle Don wanted to make sure I had a good grasp of the "dangers of overimmunization" defense he was going to hone in on. So we rehearsed. I managed to smile and nod and say all the right words, but they sounded as hollow and far away to me as my uncle's. No matter how we presented them, the "facts" still seemed inconclusive and unconvincing to me, reinforcing my conviction that recklessness—not rectitude—caused my dog's demise, a young girl's death, Emily and Doug's defection, and the end of life as I knew it.

We reentered the courtroom, a strange pair. One was confident and eager with anticipation, the other a nerve's width from collapse. Send in the clowns, I thought. I remember putting one foot in front of the other and making it to the stand, barely, by trying to focus on Uncle Don and how much this high-profile case meant to him. Nothing any longer meant anything to me.

Yet, there I was, in the hot seat, the focal point of every pair of eyes in that courtroom. Uncle Don dove right in.

"Mr. Copeland, as a veterinarian, you obviously are aware that this state, like most states in America, requires a canine rabies booster shot once every three years. Isn't that right?"

"Yes."

"Then, can you tell me, how come, when I was a boy, my dad used to bring our dog in for her rabies shot once a year? Has the law changed, Mr. Copeland?"

"Yes. Over the years, state governments have been moving toward less frequent vaccination. One year was the norm, then two years, and now it's three."

"And now it's three. And could you tell the court why our state—and most of the other states—changed the revaccination intervals from one year to three years?"

"The laws changed because evidence was growing that the level of antibodies in a dog's blood is sufficient to protect that dog against rabies beyond three years."

"Can you be a little more specific?" Mr. Copeland.

"Well, Ronald Schultz, a veterinary immunologist at the University of Wisconsin, exposed dogs to the rabies virus seven years after vaccinating them for it ..."

"Go on ..."

"The dogs did not get sick. In fact, fifteen years after their vaccinations, he found the antibody levels in the dogs sufficient to prevent rabies."

"And is that why you failed to immunize your dog after three years?"

"That's part of the reason."

"Part of the reason? What's the other part?"

"Well, there's a growing body of evidence that veterinarians today are vaccinating dogs so often, for so many different diseases, that the dogs are becoming sick as a result."

"Sick in what way?" I could tell that Uncle Don was approaching euphoria now. By some superhuman effort I had been able to draw upon a deep-seated reserve of self-preservation and perform as scripted.

"There has been a significant rise in the occurrence of an unusual immune reaction that causes heavily-vaccinated dogs to reject their own blood. This condition is fatal. There is also strong evidence that overvaccinaton in cats generates cancerous tumors called fibrosarcomas."

"So, Mr. Copeland, if I understand your testimony correctly, you failed to revaccinate your dog not out of incompetence or neglect, but because you genuinely believed you were acting in your dog's best interests."

Without waiting for a response, my devoted attorney wheeled around to face the jury. I knew he was about to launch into a stirring summary of my testimony and paint me as some sort of Albert Schweitzer-Einstein, a saintly advocate for defenseless animals and a spunky rebel against questionable science, willing to take a stand against established practices in order to stand up for his principles.

What happened next was not premeditated. Just predestined.

"Not exactly."

I'm sure everyone in that courtroom heard me, but Uncle Don refused to.

"The fact of the matter is, Mr. Copeland should be commended, not condemned, for his ac—"

"Uncle Don ... "

He turned to me, a crease bisecting his forehead. Calling him "Uncle Don" was not in the script.

As I began speaking now, the judge, jury, the other flabbergasted onlookers, surely concluded that, in addition to my other shortcomings, I was suffering from multiple personality disorder. The outwardly cool, calm, and collected defendant who had just delivered such polished testimony had left the premises. In his place was a babbling, emotional wreck who could muster up only an embarrassingly quavering voice. But at that particular time, this was the real me.

"Uncle Don, I can't do this anymore. I thought I could ... I can't."

I was saying "uncle" all right. And everyone in the room could accept that. Everyone but my uncle.

He turned to the judge. "Your Honor, I'd like to request a short recess. The witness has been through so much, and he needs—"

"*Noooooooo!*" My mournful cry pierced the courtroom with such theatricality, no one dared interrupt me now. In one unrelenting barrage, everything I'd kept inside spilled out with my tears. "I did it. I did it. Iris Mohr is dead because I was stupid and willful and blind. I put a dog above a girl—above a human life. I murdered her. I *murdered* her. Guilty as charged."

"Matthew," pleaded my steadfast advocate, "you're ignoring all the facts you yourself just presented under oath."

"I presented hypotheses, theories, inconclusive bits of evidence—not facts. I turned them into facts to serve my selfish needs, but I'm not going to do that again, not here. I tested a hypothesis against a human life, and ... you just don't do that. And, beyond that, I saw my dog acting strangely that afternoon, and I ignored it. Please, let's end this right now. Please, I beg you. End this."

For the longest moment, he just stared at me and listened to the silence in the courtroom. Finally, he looked up at the judge. "No further questions."

❄ ❄ ❄

Much to my surprise, my courtroom histrionics worked in my favor. The spectacle of a repentant defendant undermining his own case and freely admitting his guilt under questioning by his own attorney caught the jury off guard and disarmed them.

No way were they about to send a tortured soul like myself to the slammer. They simply arranged with the Veterinary Medical Board to suspend my license for five years and determined that I would pay $8000 in restitution to be divided between the Mohr family and the Petacure Clinic. Furthermore, after viewing my performance on the stand, the Mohr family dropped their wrongful death suit against me. Such a turn of events might have convinced a more emotionally balanced individual that he wasn't such a bad guy after all. But I was in no frame of mind to accept leniency for myself.

That $8000 represented basically all the assets I had in the world, yet I still couldn't escape the feeling I was getting away with murder. Deep down, I felt I had pulled the wool over the eyes of the judge, the jury, even the Mohrs. But only one person could grant me meaningful absolution. If my actions were so abhorrent that they could negate everything I had been to Emily, then she was right and everyone else was wrong. And true love was a myth. It didn't stand a chance against human imperfection. I was as guilty as sin.

Two days after the trial ended, I impulsively determined I had to see Emily. I honestly didn't want or expect forgiveness. All I sought was her confirmation that my self-loathing was fully justified. Knowing that she shared my low opinion of myself would, in some perverse way, bring us closer together. And it would help me crystallize my new and impaired self-image. She didn't have to say she hated me. She only had to let me know that, after all was said and done, she could no longer find it in her heart to love me.

So off I hurried back to the scene of my recent humiliation. I parked around the corner. As I approached the brownstone, I noticed Mobile in the window, waiting for me. Or was it Cerberus, the hound of Hades? He ran back and forth against the width of windows, seemingly agitated and intent on warning his mistress of my impending visit.

The barking continued as I paused in the vestibule, at the foot of the stairs. My mind began racing. Maybe Emily wasn't at home. Maybe she was at Doug's. Or maybe Doug was here with her. Of course, why wouldn't they be together, basking in the afterglow of his stint as star witness? Suddenly I decided the only prudent course of action was to turn tail and run. I hauled my ass out of there so fast, Mobile probably didn't know what to make of it. Scampering back to my car, I thought I detected a few suppliant whimpers mixed in with his barks.

Very well. If I couldn't bear to let Emily mete out my final punishment, I would simply have to punish myself. Self-imposed banishment far from Priorwood seemed like the obvious choice. A new identity demanded new digs.

When I returned to my temporary lodgings, my aunt and uncle were mercifully absent. I wrote them a short, sweet note, quickly packed a couple of bags, and headed out. No specific destination. I wasn't going somewhere. I was going nowhere.

On the way there, a flashing blue neon sign caught my eye. Rocco's. An unpretentious tavern on the outskirts of the metro. Until that moment, alcohol had never been an end in itself for me. I could take it or leave it. But the sign kept winking at me. Next thing I knew, I was perched at the bar.

The bartender seemed understanding, but you can't trust anyone—he eventually cut me off. Even as I staggered out, a sobering thought managed to intrude: the criminal trial was over, but the personal trial, with its attendant tribulation, could go on indefinitely. Who knew how long the jury would be out?

Looking back on it now, I understand why Rocco's sign drew me in. The Prozac had done its job—too well. I no longer felt that uncomfortable sense of detachment from reality. On the contrary, reality was suffocating me. I had to get away, and whiskey seemed the way to go.

Shortly before daybreak, through no fault of my own, I made it to a motel. I was halfway to nowhere and half in the bag. The first thing I did when I got in the room was toss my remaining Prozac in the trash. I figured reality was way overrated.

Fishes swim. Birds fly. Dogs bark. The barkless Basenjis are severely handicapped. My heart goes out to them. Barking brings purpose to my existence. Some dogs grow to love their bark so much that they abuse it and it becomes meaningless. But if more humans could learn to trust a dog's bark, it could alter the course of their existence.

— Mobile

Chapter 8
Doug's Turn

I am not an asshole.
After the trial, I had to keep reassuring myself of that. If an unbiased appraiser of my integrity had done a cursory examination of my behavior over the preceding months, they would likely conclude that I was one. To wit, I had stolen my best friend's lover with premeditation, conspired with her to testify against him in court, and gone out of my way to keep him from finding any of this out.

But a more meticulous appraiser would probe beneath the surface. They would suspect that, as a human being, with human frailties, I probably believed I was acting in a way that would assure the greatest good for the greatest number of people. So they'd dig a little deeper. Deep enough to discover that—based on feedback from both Emily and Matt—I had every reason to assume that they were over.

In Iris, Emily had lost someone very dear to her— someone I had known quite well. Naturally, I would want to console her. And as far as my ulterior motive was concerned, I accept no blame. Love is an involuntary response. We don't *decide* to love someone, so how can anyone else claim the right to decide who we should or should not love?

Some might quibble that feeling love is one thing, but acting on it is another. True enough. But feeling love and *not* acting on it is hypocritical, not to mention difficult as hell. Knowing that Matt and Emily were kaput, why shouldn't I have acted on my feelings? If he couldn't have her, who better than his best friend and clone?

And what purpose would it have served to apprise him of the situation? By unburdening myself, I would have felt better afterwards, and he would have felt worse. Until the last possible moment, I spared his feelings. To my way of thinking, I took the high road by operating on the sly about my role in the trial and my relationship with Emily.

Maybe I had another reason for not telling him about that relationship. I myself was not totally sure what it was. Despite what Matt probably concluded the day he busted in on us at her apartment, I hadn't even slept with Emily at that point—unless you define "sleeping together" as simply falling asleep together. She wanted to proceed cautiously, and I couldn't blame her. After the trial, I thought, everything would crystallize.

Everything did crystallize, though not in the way I had hoped. Since Matt's breakdown on the witness stand, Emily seemed different to me. Now that she no longer had to be on a crusade for justice, I waited for some other passion to take its place. None did. The spark of life and flash of wit that had emanated so effortlessly from her when we first met, vanished without a trace.

These were the thoughts that hit me with a sudden, sickening jolt as I lay on Emily's bed with her one evening shortly after the trial. My doubts nearly began to push aside thoughts of her beauty and of the act we were about to consummate. If it wasn't love she was feeling, what sort of consummation would it be? It would simply be sex.

I pressed her to me. She did not resist, but not because she found me irresistible. True, she was putty in my hands. But something about her apparent resignation was very unEmily-like. Truth be told, I was coming to the painful realization that I had fallen in love with the Emily that had been in love with Matt. Another girl entirely. I resolved to get that girl back. Once we made love, I figured, everything would be alright again. Despite my ambivalence, I kissed her warmly.

At that moment, Mo began barking raucously at the living room window. You could tell a lot by the intensity of his bark. A kid going by on a bike would elicit a casual *woof-woof*. Kid walking by with a dog — *bow-wow-wow*. Kid on a bicycle with a dog on a leash running alongside — *arrrrrhuh-ruh-ruh-ruh-ruh*!!!!

But this particular outburst went further yet. Besides the barking, he was jumping up with such force, you could hear his tags clanking against the windowpane. Emily and I disengaged a bit and looked at each other with amused scowls, pretending to be inconvenienced by the interruption, but, in reality, grateful for the reprieve.

I got up off the bed for the requisite check of the situation. "What's the matter, boy, did somebody come into the building?" Looking out the window, I saw no one. As I crawled back into bed, the barking subsided. With Emily under me, I prepared to pick up where we left off. "Ya think he was trying to tell us something?" she asked.

"Mobile?"

For a fraction of a second, a sad smile may have crossed the corners of her mouth. Then she nodded and looked right through me, imploringly. Without saying a word, she said plenty.

But my feelings drowned her out. "Emily, I love you. Please, let me … love you." And I proceeded to do just that.

✳ ✳ ✳

After school the next day, I came home to find that, once again, Shela had dug an escape hatch under the fence and hightailed it over to Doglegs. The day was bright and brisk, with a definite hint of autumn in the air. I decided to walk the walk I had taken so many times before, down the block, across Webster Field, into the woods. The breeze sent the odor of dog shit to greet me. This was the new reality at Doglegs. And suddenly I wondered if the old reality had been reality at all. Maybe all along Doglegs had been just one step removed from Stepford.

Midway down the first dogleg, I spotted the unmistakable silvery mane of Snow White. She was bent over, picking up shit. And I could tell by the size of the turds she harvested that they weren't the work of the Six Arfs, who waited patiently a few feet away.

"Doing other people's dirty work again, Molly? You are quite a lady."

"Oh, I think I just clean it up because I'm afraid I'll step in it otherwise."

"Yeah, right. *That's* why you do it." Half a dozen plastic bags she had filled were sitting next to the path. I picked them up and deposited them in a nearby trash can.

"Thanks, Doug. Now who's being the good Samaritan?"

"I just do it because you're here to approve of my actions. There's a difference between doing a good deed when someone's watching and doing it when nobody's around. I'll bet, all the time you were tidying up around here, no one was around."

Snow White shrugged, and her eyes twinkled. "If a bag of poop gets thrown away in the forest and nobody sees it, does it make a difference?" Just then, Boomer, Woodman, and, yes, Shela, came running across our path. "Anyhow, someone *did* see it," she continued, directing her gaze toward the trio of trespassers.

"Yes," I said. "But they don't judge us."

"No, they don't. They accept us, warts and all."

"You really believe we can learn a lot from them, don't you?"

"Believe it? Doug, I *feel* it. I *know* it."

She looked at my look, equal parts skepticism, amusement, and genuine interest. "You have a few minutes? I'll tell you all about it."

"For you, I always have a few minutes." I motioned toward a log lying alongside the path. "Why don't you have a seat in my office?"

So we sat down on the log. Molly mostly talked, I mostly listened. Judging by the way I was transported, that log may as well have been a river-borne raft.

"I don't look to the Bible for miracles, Doug. I look to dogs for faith. The miracles are happening every day. Maybe they're too commonplace to be considered miracles."

"For instance? ..."

"That story on *60 Minutes*. This dog, Jaytee, from Manchester, England knew precisely when her mistress left work every day. They set up a video camera in the woman's living room. Whenever the woman got in her car for the drive home, the dog would move to the window and look out until the car pulled up."

"OK, so the dog had excellent hearing. Where did the owner work—a block away?"

"A forty-five-minute drive away. It's a sixth sense."

"C'mon, Molly. I watch *Animal Planet*. I've heard all the inspirational stories. The dog that detected the cancerous mole on that woman's leg, and tried to bite it off. That's just their heightened sense of smell ... cancer cells give off a different smell."

"Then how do you explain the German dog that was able to retrieve toys simply on the basis of their name?"

"A conditioned response."

"The dog was even able to match toys to words it had never heard before. That's not a conditioned response. It's a sixth sense. It's also a sixth sense when dogs are able to predict epileptic seizures in kids minutes before they happen."

"OK, you can call these things psychic phenomena if you want. I prefer to think it's just a hypersensitivity to sight and sound and motion."

"Is it? Is it a child's movements that tell a dog an epileptic seizure is imminent? Or is it the energy swirling *around* that child? That living energy all of life shares. Dogs know how to use that energy to communicate with us. I know this. I feel very certain about this."

"OK, maybe. I'll grant you a 'maybe' on that one, Molly. Because you are, after all, Snow White, the doyenne of Doglegs Park."

Molly beamed. She was old enough to know what "doyenne" meant. She was proud of that title. And proud that she had gotten me to make my concession. But I wasn't about to have the conversation end on that note.

"Here's the thing, Molly. I still don't get this religious fervor where dogs are concerned. I mean, *people* can be psychic too. Who's that one guy? Edward ... "

"Edgar Cayce?" I had no idea how much actual information was hidden beneath Molly's sunny veneer. Knowledge and intelligence. "Edgar Cayce," she continued, "shares some canine qualities. But here's the thing about dogs, Doug. They occupy a pretty special rung on the evolutionary ladder. They're evolved enough to have a brain that's configured remarkably a lot like our own. So they feel lots of the same things we do. But they still know a lot of stuff that we forgot somewhere along the way. They're not evolved enough to have added all the complex wiring that fucks us humans up. They're incapable of confusion or embarrassment or deception. They don't know how to scheme or lie or pretend."

Her thesis was interesting enough that I barely noticed the anomaly of this sweet, smiling septuagenarian casually offering up "fucks." Maybe this was her way of adapting to the gritty, post-Ozzie-and-Harriet Doglegs.

"You know that old saying," I offered, "The reason a dog has so many friends is that he wags his tail instead of his tongue."

"Yep. They don't deceive others. But equally important, they don't deceive themselves. They understand we're all just here on a short holiday. And they try to make it the most positive experience possible, for themselves and for us. You wonder why I worship them, Doug, why I put them above people? It's their innate goodness. About the only bad dogs are the ones that learn from bad people. For every dog that bites a hand, there are a million that lick a hand. Those dogs that know when an epileptic fit is coming on—they're not just jumping around and barking. They're trying to protect the kid."

Molly's rant jarred my memory. "When I was a kid, I remember seeing a picture taken during a snowstorm in Virginia. About half a dozen people were trying to push a car out of a snowbank. And one dog had jumped up behind one of those people, trying to lend a helping ... paw."

Molly grinned. "I remember that picture. And I remember another one, on the front page of the *Tribune* when I was living in Chicago. This German shepherd was lying next to the dead body of a dog that had been hit by a car. That dog kept vigil there for three days. For three days it never moved, even when it was bumped by another passing car."

"That degree of loyalty to a friend ... sometimes I think humans are incapable of it," I said. "Human relationships seem to last only by mustering up an incredible effort of the will. We're fickle by nature. We always seem to let life get in the way."

Our eyes met, then mine dropped. Maybe we were both thinking about the dynamics of my own little human triangle. After an awkward silence, I said, "Well, at least we do manage to show some loyalty to our *dogs*."

"Yes," Molly agreed. "Man's loyalty to dogs helps give me faith in man. But dog's loyalty to man — *that* gives me faith in God."

She glanced down. Lo and behold, six Yorkies were sitting obediently at her feet, waiting patiently to be leashed for the stroll home. As she stood up to leave, she casually asked, "How *is* Matt?"

Her inflection took me aback. It was virtually an admission that we had both been thinking about him. Obviously, her own sixth sense was very much intact. "Haven't heard from him. Nobody has. You know, he just picked up and left."

Molly shrugged. "Sounds like a plan." And with that she picked up and left.

Separated from my true nature, I am now a confused brute, filled with hate. The physical pain is a palpable reminder of the betrayal. But what hurts even more is the fear. I must now defend myself like my primitive ancestors. These strangers approaching my cage act friendly. But so did the other. I do not trust them.

—Tina

Chapter 9
Matt's Turn

I had to admit it. Miserable as I was, losing everything was kind of liberating. Wallowing in self-pity, comforting. Assuming a new identity, exhilarating. "Freedom's just another word for nothing left to lose" was no longer just words to a song but words to live by. Sure, my new life promised to be pathetic, but suffering itself now felt so right to me, so much what I deserved. The whiskey, my new drug of choice, felt right too. It not only made life bearable but also seemed so damn appropriate for someone living—at least metaphorically—in the gutter.

The town I decided to "settle" in, Morrissey, was one of those nondescript burgs off the Interstate, eighty miles due west of my former life—eighty miles and light years. But my stopping there probably was not random. I remembered that Morrissey was home to the Blake County Animal Shelter. Surely a veterinarian—even one as infamous as myself—could wangle some menial employment there.

Just around the corner from the shelter, I found some shelter of my own. There was a sign out in front: *Furnished efficiency apartments for rent.* That struck a chord. My life was all about efficiency now. I could move in right then and there. And this place was midway between the animal shelter and a dive called Biff's Bar 'n Grill. You can't get much more efficient than that.

That first night in the efficiency, I drank myself to sleep. I think I slept through my hangover. Around noontime, I jumped out of bed, showered, shaved, and headed down to the shelter.

When I walked in, the receptionist was chatting with a woman at the front desk. They looked my way and gave me the impression that their chat could wait until I told them my business there.

"Who would I speak to about employment opportunities here?"

"That would be me," said the woman standing near the desk. "Laura Cassidy." She extended a hand, and we shook. After I introduced myself, she led me into a little conference room and interviewed me right on the spot.

"I have to tell you upfront, Matt, the only non-voluntary position we have an opening for now would be general maintenance, and it only pays eight-forty an hour."

"Forty hours a week?"

"Yes, with opportunities for overtime, especially on the weekends."

"What are the duties?"

Laura smiled. "Well, you'd be moving the animals in and out of cages, feeding them, cleaning the cages, walking the dogs, mingling somewhat with our two-legged visitors. There's some light paperwork ... "

"Sounds good."

"Tell me a little about yourself, Matt. Have you worked at all with animals?"

The halo around this woman made me want to work alongside her. She was the anti-Dr. Nancy Ruskin. No sneer when she smiled. I guessed she was a couple of years older than myself. I'd had no idea Morrissey turned out such good-looking women. If I had met her at another time in my life, who knows. She had a sweetness and an openness about her that made me feel I could do something outlandish in our interview: I could tell her the truth. So for the next twenty minutes or so, I spilled my guts ... Petacure, S.O.S., the squirrel, Emily, Iris, Doug, the trial. When I finished, Laura discreetly pushed a Kleenex box in my direction. I wasn't crying, but I was sweating.

"Listen, Matt. You can start tomorrow. Based on your background, I'm going to see if there's any way I can bump up your salary a little. I'll have to check with—"

"Don't worry about it. I live pretty simply, and I've got enough cash to get by for a while. I just appreciate the opportunity to keep occupied and work with animals." We shook on it. And that was that.

Not a minute too soon either. As we left the conference room, the receptionist rushed up to Laura. "We've got a new arrival that you need to take a look at." Laura scurried off to check out the other new arrival. I scurried off to Biff's Bar 'n Grill.

✳ ✳ ✳

First day on the job, I met Tina. She wasn't a four-legger, and she wasn't a two-legger either.

Laura introduced us shortly after ushering me into "Cell Block Number One," where they caged the dogs. I girded myself. We'd had occasion to board dogs at Petacure, but I knew this place was as far removed from Petacure as Skid Row from Skidmore. The dogs here were different. They seemed to know they were different. Passing the cages, I heard whimpers, saw desperation, and smelled homelessness, a nauseating odor equal parts shit and piss and nap. When I'd walk past, some of the more recent arrivals would bound up and down, barking loudly for a savior. These, the ones whose spirit was not yet broken, broke my heart the most. They had no clue what most likely lay ahead. Or, if they did, they weren't about to let on.

At the end of the first corridor, the occupant of the last cage stopped me in my tracks. From the medium size, pointed ears, and marbled white, brown, and black coat, I guessed it was some sort of wirehaired terrier-Lab mix. It was lying on the ground, trembling ever-so-slightly. Its head lay on the concrete floor, in between its right front leg and the short stump that was the only remnant of its left front leg. As I stepped closer, only the dog's eyes moved, but all the way to the top of their sockets, charting my progress warily.

I'd crossed paths with a three-legged dog for the first time when I was fifteen or so. That encounter no doubt played a part in my decision to pursue veterinary medicine. That three-legged dog was a phenomenon that had instantly intrigued me. Its freak-show aspect at first sent a shiver up my spine and repelled me. But when I saw how gamely it shuffled forward, it took on a gallantry nothing short of inspirational. Though certainly aware of its handicap, that dog seemed completely oblivious to it. If only paraplegics in wheelchairs could exude this same obliviousness, this sense of normalcy. But they are too conscious of others' pity, and others are aware that their pity is compounding the problem. Self-consciousness all the way around. Handicapped dogs don't have the additional handicap of self-awareness.

But the three-legger in the cage before me was nothing like the one I remembered. Besides being physically handicapped, it was a physical wreck, with cuts and swelling visible on the head and side. No wonder it didn't move. Movement was probably painful.

"This is Tina," said Laura, confirming the name posted on the cage. The posting also stated she had just arrived the day before. "She's the dog that checked in at the end of our interview yesterday."

"What happened to her?"

"We're not sure. Someone found her yesterday staggering along the street, 'bout a half a mile from here. She could barely move. Not only is she missing a front leg, but one of her rear legs looks like it's broken. The local vet we work with only comes in once a week. I was hoping you could check her out and give us your professional opinion, Mr. D.V.M. That is, if you can get close to her without getting bit. She has an attitude. If you can't manage it, don't worry about it. We'll keep her five days, but if she's not claimed, we'll need to put her down." She turned to Tina, who seemed oblivious to what was being said. "Tina, honey, I'm afraid you're about as unadoptable as they come."

For the director of an animal shelter, Laura sometimes could sound kind of cold. It was a coping technique. She was just coping as best she could with an unfathomable world.

Later that morning, I subjected Tina to my Second Coming. As I delicately opened her cage, she didn't move a muscle, but her trembling intensified. When I reached down, she bared her teeth and emitted a low, steady growl, as if to say, "What do you want with me now?" I didn't flinch. Before her agitation had a chance to escalate, I scooped her up and set her down on an examination table in an adjoining anteroom.

The shelter had some tranquilizers on hand. I managed to pop one in her mouth and close it tightly before she was able to put my hand in it as well. For the next few minutes, I talked to her as calmly and reassuringly as humanly possible. "Sometimes bad stuff happens, Tina. We don't know why it happens, and we don't deserve it, but it happens anyway. And we need to hang in there. We need to take care of ourselves ... cause even when life becomes a nightmare ... even when you feel like you can't trust anyone anymore and nothing will ever be the same again, you have to keep believing things can only get better ... they can only get better." She had swallowed the pill all right—as for my speech, I'm not sure. And I can't say as it did me a whole lot of good either.

I muzzled her and dressed her wounds. Their random placement and variety told me they most likely did not result from an accident. Also, some of the lacerations seemed more recent than others. The lack of teeth marks—plus her trembling and hostility—convinced me that this dog had had the misfortune to get hooked up with an animal of the two-legged variety. But the missing leg might not have been the work of the abuser. I noticed that the stump had apparently been neatly sewn. The amputation might have been the result of disease rather than injury.

The biggest challenge was the right rear leg. Just by looking at it, I knew the bone was broken. But when I examined it with my bare hands, I could tell it was a clean break. The tranquilizer had kicked in by now, so I was able to try sliding the upper piece over the lower, hoping that, by some miracle, I could get it to click into place. My fear was that, in the process, one of the two pieces was going to break, and this three-legged dog would become a two-legged dog. Her only hope for adoption then would be a carnival.

Amazingly, the pieces clicked. Divesting me of my license evidently had not stripped away my veterinary skills. I bandaged the leg tightly, picked her up carefully, and returned her to her cage successfully.

Over the next five days, I took increasing interest in Tina's welfare. And I detected progress, however meager. Fortunately, she didn't want to stand up, so the break had an opportunity to heal. On the second day, I coaxed her to eat some food. By the fourth day, she allowed me to pet her without so much as a snarl.

Then came the day of reckoning. Knowing there was no adoption in sight, I had been anticipating this day with steadily growing discomfort. Seven dogs were scheduled for euthanization at 3 p.m., and Tina was at the top of the list. Thankfully, the shelter had a technician on staff who handled euthanization, so I was not expected to perform it. Of course, I had euthanized my fair share of dogs at Petacure, but for the most part these were elderly or terminally ill. And we administered our shots with some regard for the dog's dignity. There was never the sort of mass genocide typical of the Monday afternoon affairs at the shelter.

As it happened, I was responsible for bringing the dogs to the euthanization chamber. I must have been giving off some telltale vibes, because, as I cradled Tina in my arms, she was back to trembling more than ever. This world did not make sense to her anymore, and, of course, I could relate. No wonder I was bonding with her. Well, at least she would soon be out of her misery—I might have to live with mine for another half-century or more.

I handed Tina over to Sharon, the technician. But in the process, the condemned looked up at me imploringly. For a split-second, a twinkle flashed across her eyes, and I could read what it said: "You won't do this, Matt. You can't do it, for your own sake, as much as for mine."

"Never mind, Sharon."

"Huh?"

I snatched Tina back. "This one's going home with me tonight."

In my new job, I was able to keep myself occupied looking after some seventy dogs, forty cats, and assorted rabbits, hamsters, and gerbils. In my new home, it was all I could do to look after myself.

No sooner did I get home than reality came flooding in. Tina and I would sit for hours staring at each other across the floor. Neither one of us knew what the hell we were doing there. But my self-imposed banishment from the world-that-was made Tina my only friend. I'd sit there sipping my Jack Daniels, and I knew she would pass no judgment.

For the first week or so, every time I'd go to put her leash on, she'd cower as if I were going to hit her. One night, as I was lying awake bemoaning my fate, I could hear her moaning in her sleep. When I went to soothe her, she was trembling and awoke with a start. I picked her up and brought her into bed with me. She stayed next to me all that night, and every night thereafter. Whatever gets you through.

Little by little, she started acting more like a normal dog. When I'd get home from work or reach for the leash, I began to notice her tail wagging. At work, I saw very few tails wagging. I guess it's hard to wag your tail when a cage gets in the way.

My own progress was not as steady as Tina's. I'm sure it was helpful for me having to keep a routine—feed her every morning, walk her every night. But I wasn't willing to think about my next move, or even the next day. Circumstances had led me to this unexpected lifestyle, and I was content, for the time being, to just maintain the status quo. At the same time, I had a feeling that, sooner or later, life would have other plans for me.

Two blocks from my apartment was a park Tina and I would frequent. It was a far cry from Doglegs in its heyday. All the dogs stayed leashed, and the people at the other end of those leashes typically gave you a simple nod or a polite "Hi." Fine by me. I was in no frame of mind for the friendly chatter that was too often a prelude to human companionship.

On a brisk evening in late October, Tina and I were walking along the perimeter of the park. She was sniffing the bushes contentedly, losing herself in the comfortable rhythms of our new life together. All at once she looked up and stared—glared—across the street. Her mouth was contorted as repeated low-pitched snarls streamed out. My eyes quickly followed Tina's gaze to a man across the street. The beagle on his leash looked our way with interest, but the man himself seemed not to notice us. He put his dog and himself into a parked car and drove off. Only then did Tina stop snarling. And only then did I realize that this mystery man might very well have been Tina's abuser.

For a minute or two, Tina and I just stood in that spot. She was panting and, every so often, glanced up at me as if to say, "Now what?" The smells in the bushes no longer intrigued her. On the walk home, I started getting increasingly pissed at myself. Why hadn't I said something to the stranger, or at least gotten his license plate? With all the watershed changes in my life, the one constant was my natural flair for doing the wrong thing.

Why do humans who treat us right treat each other poorly? How can these two not find common ground in the beauty of this park. Around some trees, I sniff sweet mysteries the likes of which I've never smelled before. And how satisfying to add my own contribution for others down the line. But the smell of my master's blood, I can live without.

— Shela

Chapter 10
Doug's Turn

I found myself humming *Autumn in New York*. Doglegs in autumn could have inspired a composition as exhilarating. That's what I was thinking as I wandered down the main path with Shela after coming home from school on a sunny first of November.

This post-apocalyptic Doglegs now communicated a bittersweet echo of its former glory. The coolness and stillness of the air kept the stench of the dung heaps at bay, so I could focus on the color palette above. Every now and then, an oak or maple leaf floated straight down, swiftly and silently, as if not wanting to draw attention to itself. In their short lives, these leaves had seen such changes.

Over the past few weeks, Shela had become unaccustomed to having me accompany her in these woods. She'd been making the trip solo and simply frolicking with the other bolters. So on this day, when she encountered Boomer and Bubba alongside the path, she promptly and happily disappeared deep into the woods with them.

And I was alone with my thoughts of Emily. Her feelings for me, I knew, were as confused as mine for her. She was living at my house now and paying the half of the rent that Matt used to pay. But I wasn't at all sure I "had" her. I only knew I didn't want to lose whatever part of her I did have. Our relationship couldn't be rushed though. I wasn't about to take advantage of her sudden passivity and resignation. If I was going to win her, I wanted to win *her*, not some pale imitation.

Before things could progress between us, her feelings about Matt had to be resolved. His mysterious disappearance wasn't helping matters any. He wasn't answering his cell, and I suspected he'd changed the number. I'd talked to his uncle, who had told me the extent of his knowledge—that Matt had left town for some unknown destination. Vaporizing as he did, immediately after his high-minded courtroom confession, reeked of martyrdom and saintliness. He may as well have ridden off on a white horse like the Lone Ranger. Nice move, Matt. Damn.

A distant bark jarred me back into the here and now. Seeing that I was at the end of the second dogleg and

Shela was nowhere in sight, I turned onto a secondary path to seek her out. Boomer and Bubba scampered by, but no Shela. Finally, I spotted her, digging away in a patch of bare soil.

She was so intent on her little project, I don't think she noticed me until I was practically on top of her. Then she stopped what she was doing, turned to look up at me for maybe five seconds, and plopped down in the dirt she had just scooped up.

As I reached down to pat her soil-covered coat, I saw a half-buried scrap of folded paper lying next to her. After picking it up, shaking off the soil, and unfolding it, I began reading:

To Emily from Matt,
You will never have to try with me
There is no way you could ever lie to me
Every word you speak will always sound like you
Every look you give will always look like you
Every move you make will always move like you
Every touch you give will always come from you
Every thought will live inside the heart of you
Every thing you do will be a part of you

While rereading Matt's syrupy words, I leashed Shela and resumed walking. As I stuffed the crumpled note in my pocket, I felt something squish under my sneaker. Even if I hadn't been engrossed in my reading, I probably wouldn't have spotted this particular turdpie. Some freshly fallen leaves had done their best to conceal it.

When I walked into the house that night with the dogs, Mo and Shela greeted Emily, who had just gotten in from work. I immediately took my sneakers off and set them by the door. "I just stepped in some shit at Doglegs."

Emily didn't respond. As soon as I saw her, I knew she had something on her mind. She seemed distracted and slightly ill-at-ease. The dogs lingered with us in the living room.

"What's the matter?" I asked.

"A lot."

"What happened?"

"A child happened."

"Huh?"

"Our child, Doug … growing in my belly, as we speak."

She smiled her sweetest sad smile. She was so good at those smiles, so good at conveying her feelings without actually articulating them. What she was conveying just then was, "This is a wonderful thing, if only the circumstances were different."

I chose to ignore that last part. What she lacked in enthusiasm, I more than made up for. In terms of solidifying our relationship, this pregnancy was my ace-in-the-hole, so to speak. "I'm not exactly sure how this happened," I said. "But I'm so glad it did. Are *you*? I mean, we're going to keep our baby, right?" Emily seemed to notice that I said "we're" and "our."

She sat down on the sofa. "Well, apparently it was meant to be."

"You're damn right it was meant to be," I said, taking my partnerly place next to her on the sofa.

"It did happen kind of out of the blue though."

"No, not out of the blue. In the blue. Did you see a doctor? When is it due?"

"Late June."

"Listen, I know what you've been through this year, cause I've been through it with you. I know you've got to be confused. But, look at me. Everything is going to work out okay. Do you trust me? Listen, if you want marriage ... a wedding ... now ... later ... I don't care. Honey, whatever you want."

She studied me and, as the seriousness of my intentions registered, began to sob. From way deep down, the way opera singers sing, that's how she sobbed. "Oh, Doug, I don't know what I want." She threw her arms around me, and I could feel her entire body sobbing. At that moment, I couldn't be sure if I was an object of affection or comfort or pity.

When she finally settled down and mopped up her face, she seemed to regain her composure. "There is one thing I want."

"Just name it."

She hesitated. "I want you to find Matt."

"Huh?"

"Doug, he was your best friend. Don't you want to talk to him, see how he's doing ... try to put all this behind us and still be friends? The trial was so ... uncomfortable."

Uncomfortable? It was uncomfortable like a thousand lashes with a whip are uncomfortable. I agree with you. I think it would do us all good to get some sort of closure. But I don't think he's in town."

She stood up. I'm not sure that her fists were actually clenched at her sides, but that's the impression I remember from her body language. "If he ever found out about this baby from someone else, it would just … I don't know. Just find him, okay?"

She looked beautiful in her misery. The classic tragic heroine. "Emily, I love you. I've loved you from the start, when I wasn't supposed to love you. And maybe I'm not supposed to love you now, not as long as this—this thing—is hanging over both of us. I will find Matt."

✳ ✳ ✳

So I paid an awkward visit to the home of Matt's aunt and uncle. Mercifully, Uncle Don wasn't there. Aunt Maura was a lot less adversarial.

"Oh, dear!" she exclaimed. "I don't think I can tell you where he is, because we don't know ourselves."

"You haven't heard from him? No letters?"

"Well, we did get one, but it didn't say a whole lot. He did tell us he had adopted a little dog." Opening a drawer in the dining-room buffet, she produced the letter, envelope and all. She glanced at it. "I'm afraid it doesn't have a return address on it."

But I did see the postmark on it. Morrissey. This nugget of information would be intelligence enough to earn me some brownie points with Emily. "OK, well, thank you anyway."

✳ ✳ ✳

The next day was Saturday. With Shela in the seat next to me, I drove the eighty-something boring minutes to Morrissey. I passed most of the time in a futile effort to rehearse just what it was I was going to say to the fugitive, if and when I did find him.

I figured that, if Matt had adopted a dog, it was even money he had gotten it from the Blake County Animal Shelter. So Plan A was to locate him through the shelter. On the one hand, I wondered what I was going to do if Plan A failed. On the other, I worried about what I was going to do if Plan A *didn't* fail. I simply hoped for the best, realizing full well that this was the plan of attack employed by the Captain of the *Titanic*.

Driving down Morrissey's Main Street, I noticed the dime store, the barbershop, the American Legion hall. Despite its 70,000 population, Morrissey had a small-town—almost a ghost-town—feel. Apologies to Mr. Mellencamp, but I couldn't imagine myself living in a small town. I couldn't imagine Matt living there. Not the Matt I'd known.

Pulling into one of the cattywampus parking spaces near the animal shelter, I went inside to do my detective work. At the front desk, I asked if I could find out if they had records of a certain person adopting one of their dogs.

"Sir, I'm afraid we're not allowed to give that information out."

To make sure she knew I was aggravated, I rubbed my forehead and sighed. "Listen, l have good reason to believe that a Matt Copeland adopted one of your dogs, and I need to speak with him. He's an old friend of mine."

She brightened. "Oh, you're friends with Matt?" Obviously, this *was* a small town. "He works here."

"Really! Well, could I speak with him?"

"Oh, I think he's off today. Um, but he just lives a little ways from here."

Evidently, any friend of Matt's was a friend of hers, because, without any prodding on my part, she gave me directions to his apartment. Before she could realize she'd breached security procedures, I said, "Thanks," and went on my way.

Enroute to Matt's, I spotted a park. I decided I'd walk Shela there first, because she was getting a little antsy. So was I. Anything that would delay the imminent confrontation seemed like a plan.

No sooner had we started walking than Shela stopped in her tracks. She stared for a moment at something in the distance and remained immobilized, except for her twitching nose. Then she lunged forward with such force that I had to let go of the leash to keep from falling and being dragged on the ground behind her.

All I could make out was the indistinct figure of a man with a small dog at the far end of the park. Even before I could positively confirm what Shela had seen or heard or smelled, I sensed, at some level, it had to be Matt. I walked tentatively after Shela, who was light-years ahead of me. While she traversed the mammoth park in maybe fifteen seconds, I might as well have been on the Bataan Death March.

I recognized Matt's form as he teased his dog with a tennis ball, but he only threw it a few yards. That's when I noticed the dog was missing a leg. It gamely ran-hopped after the ball. Just then Matt's side-vision caught my charging hound. Too late. Shela barreled into him, knocking him off his feet. From my gradually improving vantage point, I watched the reunion unfold. Shela was all over Matt. His own dog, returning from its tennis ball retrieval, dropped the ball and stared in bemusement.

Matt glanced over in my direction just long enough to learn who it was, then continued cavorting with the dogs. Clearly, he had no intention of making this any easier for me.

I watched as he scooped up his dog, and, still sitting on the ground, introduced it to Shela. Then he lay down on the grass and bench-pressed his dog up in the air, letting Shela know that this was a friend, and letting his dog know that the interloper was not about to jeopardize its place with him. Finally, I saw him formally introduce his dog to mine.

As I approached closer, Shela ran halfway to me and back again—she wanted to make damn sure I didn't miss the surprise in store for me. Matt just continued devoting all his attention to the dogs. When I was an arm's length away, he was still on the ground. He looked up at me with no fathomable expression. And not one word. Even a "Well, what brings you here?" might have helped break the ice, though I'm not sure how I would have responded.

I spoke first. "How are you, Matt? ... Sorry, I'm an idiot. I know how you must be."

He smiled. "Unless you're living it, you don't know. Actually, I'm doing alright right now. Got someone to love, someone who loves me." He stroked his dog. "This is Tina. Pretty special. She's the three-legged wonder." Tina looked up, as if to matter-of-factly confirm, "Indeed, I am."

Matt eyed me with a snide smile. "Where's Emily? I'm surprised you two didn't come together." He paused. "Wouldn't be surprised if you two are coming together a lot these days." Another pause, more uncomfortable than the first. Matt had lost a lot, but not his acerbic way with words.

"Maybe I shouldn't have come at all," I offered.

"Sit down, Doug." He commanded it as though he were talking to a dog. I obeyed. So did Tina, who may have thought he said, "Sit down, dog."

Rather than continuing the conversation, I tried to restart it. "Matt, the two of us ... we've both done things we've ... regretted."

"Yeah, like meeting here today."

He was letting it all out now, and I tried to ignore it. "What's happened, happened. But we can change the future. Why don't you come home?"

"Come home? To what? A woman who loved me once upon a time? A best friend who moved in on that woman when he should have been standing by me?" He kept stroking Tina as he spoke. "I don't need to go home. I'm at home right here. That other world—it isn't working for me anymore."

I looked away to see Shela thirty yards away, checking out the scents next to a couple of trees and oblivious to the drama now unfolding. I turned back to Matt. "We're only human. We're unpredictable. We change. We build these unrealistic expectations of each other. But stuff happens. Life happens."

Matt nodded, stood up, and looked down on me. "You sound like you're speaking for Emily now."

"She's the one who wanted me to find you, Matt. She's so worried about you. Part of her is always going to belong to you, Matt."

"Seems I'm no longer majority stockholder though. Think I oughta try for a hostile takeover?"

"Emily is having a pretty tough time of it, Matt." To complicate things further, she ... uh, just found out she's pregnant."

"No kidding? Who's the proud papa? Anyone I know? Gee, you suppose it's me? She about six months pregnant?"

His cold sarcasm was making me feel so small, I decided to stand up as well. He was unrelenting. "Guess this is what they call a pregnant pause."

"If it makes you feel any better, Matt, I feel like a schmuck."

"No, that doesn't make me feel any better." As he was speaking, his fist came at me from out of nowhere. On the word "better," it delivered a knockdown blow, centered between my nose and my eye. In twenty-some years of knowing him, nothing had prepared me for it. And I'm not gonna lie—it hurt like hell. As I lay there, flat on my back, I managed to open one eye and see him standing over me. "*That* does," he said. Because you *are* a schmuck."

Shela trotted over to sniff the blood trickling from my nostril. Then she calmly sniffed Matt, as if to confirm that he had been responsible. He stalked off with Tina. Shela absent-mindedly tagged along in his general direction. Her tail was way down.

"Shela!" The urgent tone in my voice brought her back. I dabbed the blood from my nose with my hanky and managed to get myself to my feet. As I trudged back to the car, my tail was between my legs as well. The ill-conceived "peace talks" were officially over.

They smell exactly the same. Until now, I had forgotten how comforting those scents could be. The hurt may never leave me, but I must bury it at the bottom of the black hole in my past. These people will see no signs of the wounded Tina, and I must try to forget her. But I have learned how transient happiness can be.

— Tina-Bonita

Chapter 11
Matt's Turn

Where had I ever learned a right hook like that? I'd never thrown a punch in my life. I'd thrown a party once, and spiked the punch. That had been about the extent of my troublemaking capacity.

All my life I'd been Mr. Nice-Guy, and everybody knows nice guys finish last. Finally, I knew it too. All of a sudden, it felt macho to be mean. It felt good to be bad. I didn't have much, but I had my pride, goddammit.

This new Matt felt dangerous and sexy. I was twenty-eight years old, and I'd only actually fucked four women, all of them "nice" girls. That night I was going to take me home a bad girl. A bad girl for a bad guy. Tina'd understand. Tina'd seen it all.

In the evening I took a shower, got all the Doug smell off of me. I decided not to shave, but that didn't stop me from slapping on the last of the after-shave I'd bought, back when I had money to buy things like after-shave.

When I was all duded up, Tina came over to kiss my fragrant cheek. I whispered, "Wish me luck," in her mangy ear, then headed down to Biff's Bar 'n Grill.

Biff's was the type of tavern that could become a second home to a man like me. At 9 p.m., the place was hopping. There was no piano, but *Piano Man* was playing on the jukebox when I walked in, and this was the sort of desperate-to-be-happy place that could have inspired the song.

I'm not sure how long Jack Daniels and I sat at the bar, but, as the hour grew later, he managed to convince me that the dark-complexioned lady—chatting with two other ladies at the table behind me—was more sultry looking than she had previously appeared. Her breasts were exposed just enough to leave something to the imagination. So I imagined.

Down the bar a-ways, the poor bartender was politely listening to some drunken lout who'd been talking nonstop ever since I walked in. I wanted to get away from his aggravating tirade. So when Joni Mitchell started singing *Help Me* on the jukebox, I decided to help myself. Determined to experience some sexual healing, I got up from my stool.

I walked over to my about-to-be lady friend and asked if I could buy her a dance. She was warm and willing, and then some. After no more than ten seconds on the dance floor, we were old pals, our arms entwined around each other, our bodies bonded together like flypaper. Any actual dance steps were almost incidental—who needs to feel the music when you're feeling each other? This was even easier than my initial get-acquainted session with Emily back at Doglegs. I was thinking to myself that I had to start getting out more often.

The tiny dance floor was closer to the loudmouth at the bar than my vacated barstool was, and he was sounding louder than ever. When I got a good look at him, a vaguely uncomfortable feeling started gnawing at me. I knew I'd seen this bozo before. Even though I couldn't remember where or when, his appearance brought back some sort of unpleasant association. I wracked my brain trying to think where this character and I had crossed paths. The animal shelter? The trial? The possibilities started spinning around in my brain, along with the whiskey.

By now I was resenting this guy simply because he had jarred me out of my carnal euphoria. No longer was I able to tune out his torrent of nonsensical words. I began to hear complete thoughts.

"What a stupid ingrate. I feed her, give her a roof over her head, and the first chance she gets, she tries to run away from me. So I start runnin' after her, yellin' after her. She just keeps hoppin' away … pathetic three-legged bitch. Well, when I catch up with her, I just lost it, man. I throw her around, whack her but good. Ungrateful mutt. I tried dragging her for a little while on the leash, but she was, like, dead weight. I finally figured, what the hell do I need some dumb-ass, three-legged bitch anyhow, so I just left her there."

We had danced over to where this guy was sitting, and I managed to extricate myself from my dance partner's arms. "Excuse me," I said in my most charming manner. "I couldn't help overhearing. Was this a fox terrier type dog, black and brown and white?"

The second he started to nod his head, I felt a rage wash over me, and it unleashed a fury probably not unlike what this imbecile had let loose on Tina.

His face, which might have appeared altogether normal to the casual observer, began transforming into evil incarnate through the prism of my reflections. Instantly it morphed into a succession of hideous images—Doug's awkward glance the day I'd barged in on him and Emily, the insensitivity of Petacure's Nurse Ratchet, the darting eyes of a crazed white squirrel. I swear, for one fleeting instant, it took on the form of a highly magnified rhabdovirus I could remember all too well from my vet school lab.

Out came my late-blooming right hook. My adversary went down like a ton of bricks. With Doug, one punch had satisfied my blood lust. But the sight of this monster lying on the floor before me just fueled my anger. As I pulled him up by his shirt collar and laced into him again and again, I felt like an avenging angel.

Then I felt something else. A powerful pair of hands grabbed me from behind and twisted my arms behind me. In short order, a second pair of hands slapped handcuffs on my wrists. Unbeknownst to me, Biff's was a popular hangout for plain-clothes cops.

So there I was, Matthew Copeland—recent D.V.M., model citizen, and all-around goody two-shoes—escorted to a prison cell for the second time in seven months. But whereas I had been in a state of shock the first time around, I now felt in a state of grace. I had become a stoic crusader, unfazed by an insane world which could no longer let me down, so low were my expectations.

Well, once again I had the luxury of my very own cell, with a cot in the corner. Not too shabby. But just ten minutes after my arrival, my mercifully solitary confinement ended abruptly when the warden opened my cell door to usher in the archetypical town derelict with the simple directive, "In ya go, Martin." I never did find out if Martin was the poor bastard's first name or his last. Maybe he was such a frequent visitor that he and the staff were on a first-name basis.

Martin was textbook—ruddy checks dotted with pockmarks, handlebar mustache drooping asymmetrically, breath reeking of cheap wine and halitosis. This odor combined with the B.O. oozing from his every pore to create an Essence of the Gutter that made me wish Tina was there. Any dog would think they had died and gone to heaven.

He looked me up and down and mumbled, "Why you here?"

"Oh, I don't know," I answered. "Probably the same reason you are—disturbing the peace."

"They disturbed *my* peace," he snarled. At least that's what I thought he said. But we wasn't talking about peace. "A guy can't take a piss in this town anymore. Where the fuck are you supposed to go when the restaurants won't let you in and the fucking office buildings lock their bathrooms?"

"So they hauled you in for taking a leak on the street?"

He sighed and suddenly seemed very tired. "Oh, I gave 'em hell. Shit. I should've just walked away."

"Oh, so you got pissed off cause they wouldn't let you get your piss off." That's what I would have said if I'd been talking with anyone who could appreciate my stupid puns. But too many of this fellow's brain cells had died a premature death, including the ones capable of pun appreciation. And yet, I could detect a hint of intelligence in his deep-set eyes.

"How had Martin started out?" I wondered. What secret did he and Fate share? Was he dealt all the wrong cards at birth or did he—like his cellmate—hit a rough patch in the road along the way and tumble down a cliff?

"Shoulda walked away," he repeated. As he spoke these words, he started walking away, almost as if trying to show me that he did indeed know how to do the right thing but had simply neglected to do it. He staggered over toward the cot, walking in a circular motion but somehow getting to his destination and plopping down on his back. I had the feeling he had been there before.

The cell was chilly. I walked over to the cot, picked up the modest blanket draped over one end, and threw it over Martin. As I stood over him, he began to snore, turning up the volume with each release of breath. I wondered if he dreamed. I wondered *what* he dreamed. And how many years had he taken to arrive at this sorry state? Studying him then, I hadn't a clue whether he was sixty years old or forty.

I saw a guard walk by and thought to call out, "Excuse me, there's only one cot in here, and it's taken. Where do I sleep?"

"Yeah, we're more crowded than usual tonight. I can probably scare something up for you." He walked off and came back a minute later with a pillow and blanket but no cot. Maybe they expected me to snuggle up next to my new crony.

I set the pillow down on the floor in the corner furthest from the cot, then I set myself down. I figured the shortage of accommodations was a good sign; they'd probably turn me loose in the morning. Anyhow, I had to smile at the thought of how far and how fast I had fallen. It was a secure feeling. Once you've hit bottom, there's only one way to go.

The game of life was making me feel like a kid, because this game seemed nothing more than *Candyland*. One minute you're approaching Ice Cream Floats, the next you're hit with a Cherry Pitfall.

From the opposite corner, the snoring continued unabated. To drown it out, or maybe to complement it, I started humming myself to sleep with *The Midnight Special*. Yeah, I was a bad, bad man alright.

Next thing I knew, the warden was waking me up and escorting me down the hallway. He said it was high noon, and the deputy sheriff wanted to talk to me.

❅ ❅ ❅

The warden motioned for me to sit down at a chair next to a tidy desk. On the desk sat a nameplate that read, *William Tompkins Deputy Sheriff*. Behind the desk sat the man himself.

There's day and night. Black and white. Wrong and right. And then there's Martin and Tompkins. Where Martin had been buffeted about by life, wandered aimlessly through it, and viewed it simply as an unfeeling waiting room (if he viewed it at all), Tompkins operated on the premise that life was home. He was comfortable enough in it to have made it his castle.

Of course, I wasn't consciously thinking all this at the time. But reflecting on it now, I remember him instantly giving off this vibe of being fully engaged with life. Something about him put me at ease. Maybe it was the devotion in the eyes of the German shepherd sitting on the floor next to him.

"Nice dog," I said. "He work here?"

"Gus is our most dedicated employee. Sniffed out a dope ring over in Burlington just a few weeks ago."

"Oh, yeah. I read about that." I patted Gus, who gave me a "What's-a-nice guy-like-you-doing-in-a-place-like-this" stare. "Good going, Gus."

"I'll bet you were a helluva veterinarian."

I looked up from the dog with a start. "Apparently, you're a helluva detective."

He smiled. "Thanks to Google, anyone can be a good detective these days. I read about your trial online. The reporter seemed to think you got a raw deal."

"Maybe, maybe not. Anyway, reporters don't carry as much weight as lawyers."

"I talked to the bartender at Biff's, so I understand what triggered your assault last night. I also talked to Laura Cassidy over at the animal shelter."

"Guess it must have been kind of a slow day at the office." Uh-oh. Maybe I was coming across a little too flip. I laughed nervously. I didn't want to antagonize the man with the badge. But he was cool.

"Laura told me all about you and Tina. I'm the one who found Tina, half-dead. I brought her into the shelter about the same time you started there."

Realizing that this stranger had a grasp on everything I'd been through, I could feel the gratitude welling up in me and coming out in the form of a single tear that trickled down my cheek. So much for my hardened criminal facade.

Good detective that he was, Tompkins saw the tear. He also saw that I saw he saw it. "You gonna stay in Morrissey the rest of your life, or are you going home?"

"This is home now."

"If you're gonna rebuild your life, maybe you oughta confront your demons head on."

"I thought I'd be getting a tongue-lashing from a deputy sheriff. Turns out, you're not only a detective— you're a shrink."

"Makes my job more interesting. Jailbirds of your caliber don't come along every day, you know. Listen, Matt, I know all about the case ... about your girlfriend, about her niece. I know the whole story."

"The paper didn't tell the whole story. It didn't tell how the girlfriend is now living with my ex-best friend and having my ex-best friend's baby."

For once, Tompkins didn't seem quite so in command. "Well, these things have a way of working themselves out. Just be patient."

"Oh, I'm very patient. Notice that I haven't even asked you when I'm getting out of here. Or *if* I'm getting out."

"We're letting you out of here right now, but with two conditions attached." He paused, as if to indicate the gravity of what he was about to say. "You'll have to come back here to do more time."

"Huh?"

"About half an hour." He grinned broadly.

"Let's see ... Deputy Sheriff, detective, psychiatrist, comedian ... kind of a Renaissance man, aren't you?"

Tompkins brushed aside the compliment. "In a couple of days, I want you to look through our files ... see if you recognize our dog abuser. I'd have you do it now, except our mug-shot book is getting digitized."

"Oh, I'll definitely be back for that. What's the second condition?"

"Well, in addition to all my other credentials, I'm the husband of an ace reporter. My wife works over at the *Morrissey Morning Sun*. I just spoke to her. She wants to do a feature on you. She'll be calling you, and we expect you to cooperate fully."

"No problem, Sheriff. And thank you."

"OK, now get out of here. And keep your fists to yourself. I don't want to see your mug behind bars again."

Gus heaved a contented sigh and laid his head down on his front paws. But his eyes stayed glued to me as I stood up. I patted him again, gave Tompkins a heartfelt handshake, and walked. I guess, as prisons go, the one I'd created for myself on the outside would suffice. I'd leave this one to Martin.

Angela Tompkins and her *Morning Sun* did a story on me that had me sounding like the love-child of Ralph Nader and Mother Teresa. And the big photo they included of the excommunicated veterinarian and his three-legged dog did not go unnoticed.

One day after the story ran, the receptionist at the shelter called me away from my morning feedings to say a Mrs. Sanchez was up front and needed to speak to me. When I sat down with her on a bench in the reception area, she began speaking haltingly, carefully, in broken English. "I see the story about you in the newspaper ... you and Bonita."

Bonita and Tina, I then learned, were one and the same. The Sanchez family had adopted Bonita as a puppy, a four-legged one. At the age of three she developed cancer, resulting in amputation of her left front leg. Several months later, ten-year-old Kyle Sanchez went out to the fenced-in backyard to play with Bonita, only to find she had disappeared without a trace.

Her apparent abduction was gut-wrenching for the family. Mrs. Sanchez told me that, after the operation, she and her husband and three children had grown even closer to Bonita than before. They saw themselves as her protectors, and vice versa. "Mr. Copeland, I know Bonita is now your friend. But, my Linda, sometimes she is still crying herself to the sleep at night."

I held up my hand to indicate that she did not need to say another word. "I will bring Bonita back to you tonight. About seven?"

"Oh, thank you so much. Yes, seven is very good."

At seven that night, Bonita, a.k.a. Tina, reunited with her family in the most heartwarming scene since *Lassie Come Home*. Tina-Bonita actually moaned in bittersweet delight as she hopped from Linda to Kyle, and mama and papa cozied up to her as well. They also made it clear I was their hero, serving up bottomless portions of tortilla chips, salsa, and the best sangría I'd ever experienced. This was a serious celebration.

As the Sanchez clan made up for lost time with Bonita, I looked at their family pictures on the wall. This was a good home for Bonita, for any dog. In between two framed photos of Bonita, one pre-cancer and one post, was a smaller frame with an inscription on it. I read the words, and the sap in me rose.

And, beloved master, should the great Master see fit to deprive me of my health or sight, do not turn me away from you. Rather hold me gently in your arms as skilled hands grant me the merciful boon of eternal rest ... and I will leave you knowing with the last breath I drew, my fate was ever safest in your hands.

"A Dog's Prayer"
by Beth Norman Harris

Yes, this was a good home. All I could think of was how much Snow White would love to have that hanging in her home. Maybe it already was. Heck, I wouldn't be surprised if Beth Norman Harris was her pseudonym.

Before I left, I did have one question for the Sanchezes. "Any idea who might have taken Bonita from you?" Without saying a word, Mr. Sanchez stepped into another room and returned with a small paper bag. He handed it to me, and I looked inside to find a crumpled, monogrammed hanky. "It was in the backyard the day Bonita disappeared," he explained.

I tried to imagine someone buying monogrammed hankies for a dog-beating psychopath. "Mind if I take this with me?" I asked.

"That's fine." Bonita for a soiled hanky—he had to love that trade.

I thought of letting Tina-Bonita sniff the hanky, then thought better of it. Why ruin a happy occasion? I stroked her one last time. She knew she wouldn't be going home with me. We were both sad, and very happy. The sadness was less disconcerting for me than the happiness. I had forgotten what happy felt like. It was almost more than I could handle. But Tina seemed to have no problem adapting to her good fortune. Dogs are engineered for happy.

Next day, I made my way to the Deputy Sheriff's office, this time on my own recognizance. When I showed Tompkins the monogrammed hanky, he nodded approvingly and led me to his computer.

Determined to match the hanky's embroidered *NLV* to a familiar face on file with the law, I hit the jackpot within two minutes: Nicolai Leon Virostek. No mistaking those deceptively normal features. Under the photo was a description of an earlier crime: petty larceny. But now we could get him for grand theft—provided the judge understood there was nothing "petty" about the value of a dog like Bonita to a family like the Sanchezes.

Tompkins was ecstatic. I have a feeling, had I never even paid him a visit, eventually he would have tracked down Virostek on his own. After sheepishly advising me that the address he had for Virostek was probably not current, he called the Blake County Hospital—local police had taken my "victim" to the emergency room there the night of my arrest. The hospital had an address for him. It was just a mile away. I begged Tompkins to let me join the posse, but he would have none of it. "I'll have another officer along, and Gus will be with us."

"If you're taking Gus, take this." I gave Tompkins the hanky. A few minutes later, the Deputy Sheriff and his partners—human and canine—hopped in a squad car and sped off.

Sometimes things happen fast in a small town. Just a couple of hours later, Tompkins called me at the shelter to tell me they had Virostek in custody. And the hanky had come in handy. The building directory listed no apartment numbers, but after giving Gus one whiff of the hanky, Deputy-Sheriff's best friend led the officers right to Virostek's door. The culprit offered no resistance. Apparently, he felt more comfortable confining his episodes of violence to situations involving three-legged dogs.

Not only had Tompkins taken a menace off the streets, but now he'd be able to give his wife a follow-up exclusive on the Tina-Bonita drama. I guess, once in a while, nice guys do finish first. As for me, I had the distinct pleasure of trying to imagine Virostek sharing a cot with Martin.

The earth beneath my paws comes up quickly. To dig is to experience unlimited possibility. Another world exists below, and who knows what I might find there? I also dig to create—to form a temporary dwelling where I can feel cold soil beneath my belly. But there is a third reason I dig. I dig because she asks it.

— Mobile

Chapter 12
Emily's Turn

For any one of us, reality can have multiple layers. As December rolled around, I added on a top layer designed to keep me snug and secure. This was the reality that told me everything just might work out okay. I had a baby on the way, a job that I loved, a decent guy who loved me. My protective outer layer allowed me to go about business as usual and live my everyday life. I wasn't about to screw any of that up.

But when I went to bed at night, the top layer came off. And the fabric underneath wasn't very attractive. It didn't go with anything—just a clashing hodgepodge of what-might-have-beens and never-could-have-beens.

Maybe that's why I kind of looked forward to the sex with Doug at night. It provided a momentary respite from the discomfort of being alone with my thoughts. But as soon as Doug rolled away, everything came flooding back. And increasingly my internal monologue was spilling over onto my tongue—and into Doug's ears.

"I never thought I'd be that woman."

Doug's response was perfunctory, automatic. He sounded like he was anticipating the answer to his question before he even asked it. "What kind of woman is that?"

"The woman who dumps her boyfriend for his best friend."

"Well, your situation wasn't exactly typical."

"Oh, please. Every girl thinks her situation is atypical. There doesn't have to be a death involved, or a trial."

"Hey, I'm not talking about all that. That's not what makes your situation special." He grabbed me and pulled me close. "*This* is." He kissed me as if he believed that, but it was too soon for a reprise of what we'd just finished. His spirit was willing, but not his body.

I slid away from him. "We still haven't settled things with … "

" … with Matt. Not that again, I beg you. We did settle things. Matt settled things. He settled his fist into my nose, which, by the way, is just beginning to stop hurting."

"Wouldn't you like your child to know him?" Wrong thing to say. Now I'd succeeded in getting him good and angry.

"Not particularly. It's not my goal for Matt and I to become the Bruce Willis and Ashton Kutcher of

Priorwood, Demi. And I don't think all this is about me and Matt getting chummy again ... I think it's about you getting Matt back in your life. Maybe he never left." Doug turned away and took most of the covers with him.

"I'm sorry. I won't say any more about it."

"I'm sorry too. I was under the misguided impression that, after having sex, women liked to bask in the afterglow, not wallow in the past. I'll just give you the benefit of the doubt and say it's your pregnancy hormones acting up."

"I've finished wallowing. Go to sleep, honey."

He went right to sleep. I went back to wallowing. I wallowed past 11 p.m., past midnight, past one in the morning. And when I grew tired of lying in bed wallowing, I got up and did the walking wallow. Pacing back and forth, I thought about how much I hated the woman I had become. I hated the things I said. If I were Doug, I wouldn't have moved to the other side of the bed but to the other side of the world.

Curled up on the floor, Shela and Mo had their eyes wide open, watching my every move. As I patted them, I was thinking that this living-with-two-realities business was easier said than done. Dogs got it right. They have only one reality. Their outer and inner lives blend together seamlessly. No wonder so many canine psychiatrists are starving.

Apparently, my restlessness had gotten to Mobile. He plodded over to the door and started scratching. He wanted to join some of his friends at Doglegs. At any hour, day or night, at least half a dozen dogs were sure to be there. I opened the door, and he scooted off without a backward glance.

Shela got up, stretched, walked over to the computer in the corner of the room and settled down on the floor next to it. Without conscious motive, I followed her over there. The computer was in the Sleep mode. If only sleep were that easy for me. I absentmindedly plunked down on a key, and the sudden brightness of the screen startled me.

Seeing the Google search box in front of me, I took a seat and typed "Matt Copeland" almost without thinking. If somebody had seen me as the search items came up, they'd have instantly understood how Google got its name. I was googly-eyed. Above the familiar links to newspaper articles dealing with Iris's death and the trial, I found listings from the *Morrissey Morning News*, links to Matt's new life. After gobbling up every last word, I knew sleep was hopeless.

So I hopped into a pair of jeans and loafers, threw on Doug's old jacket, and leashed Shela. Like Patsy Cline, I suddenly felt the urge to "go out walkin' after midnight."

Doug was a sound sleeper, but my hustle-and-bustle woke him just as I was headed out the door. "Emily? What are you doing? It's almost two in the morning."

"I can't sleep. And Mo's down at Doglegs. I'm going to take Shela to the edge of the park and see if I can call him."

"Oh, Mo's always down at Doglegs. He'll be fine. And we've got work in the morning. And you've got our child in your womb."

"Well, if I take Shela out now, we can sleep a little later this morning."

Doug groaned, and I masked the sound with my door slam. The night air felt wonderful. The wind was swirling snow flurries every which way—typical early December in Priorwood. I held both leashes in one hand so I could warm the other one in Doug's coat pocket. That's when I felt the crumpled ball of paper. A note from school, I imagined: "Please excuse Jane from class yesterday as she had a sore throat."

As I opened the paper, a cloud unveiled a full moon, and I was able to see Matt's lost declaration with complete clarity. Shela could have suffered whiplash, so suddenly did I stop. I unleashed her, and she headed off to join Mobile and God-knows-who-else.

Reading the words, I felt them reverberate through me as though coming from some far-off echo chamber. But the echo was soon drowned out by a volley of questions. Why was this in Doug's pocket? Where did he get it? How long had he had it? And, the $64,000 question: why hadn't he given it to me?

My mind started racing, and my legs followed. Suddenly I felt a powerful pull toward Doglegs. Whatever peace the dogs were finding there, I wanted some of that for myself.

The flurries grew heavier, the air colder. When I entered Doglegs, Shep the Border collie ran up, not so much to greet me as to herd me. For some reason that was not for me to know, he did not want me on the main path. Instead, he nudged me over to the right. Then he turned into a narrow path, ran ten paces up it and five paces back, repeating this routine to make sure I followed him.

I came to the "hallowed ground" where Matt and I had holed up together one magical morning the past April. Immediately, I knew what I had to do. Getting down on my knees, I began scooping up the earth. This time I would bury that note so deep, no one would ever again find it.

As I dug, Shela, Mobile, and some of the other "locals" stepped out from the darkness. I recognized Woodman and Bubba and Cora, who was now fully grown. When I hit rock bottom, I laid out the note and began covering it with the earth I had just dug up. Much to my amusement, Shela and Mo put their hind legs to work and started helping me.

But before the job was complete, I noticed all the dogs acting a little fidgety—Shep in particular. Now he was trying to herd me back in the opposite direction. "Shep, what am I going to do with you? You are one mixed-up puppy."

He was barking at me now, insistently, and other dogs were joining in. They seemed agitated. Woodman was howling. Bubba was licking me. And Mobile grabbed the bottom of my jacket and tried to pull me from the scene. But they could not deter me from my obsession with completely filling in the hole and packing down the dirt.

With the job finally finished, I looked up through the branches of an old oak tree to see the moon still playing hide-and-seek with the clouds. The majesty of that moment is forever commingled with terror in my memory, for that was when I finally realized what the dogs had known minutes earlier. An ominously low crackling now accompanied the howling of the wind. Before I could take two steps, the oak crashed down as if it had eyes—eyes for me.

It could have killed me a dozen different ways, but the only part of the main trunk to hit me was the upper portion, where it was no more than five inches in diameter. Still,

I was pinned under it, with the small of my back bearing the brunt. Since I was face down and branches lay over my head, I couldn't see much. But I could hear the dogs around me.

As I lay there, not knowing if I were going to live or die, I thought of a book that had affected me deeply as a canine-crazed high-school sophomore: *Kinship With All Life* by J. Allen Boone. The book told the ostensibly true account of the author's incredible dog-sitting experiences with Strongheart, the German shepherd who had gained world renown in the 1920s as a canine motion-picture star.

While sharing his home with Strongheart, Boone learned how to communicate with the dog by not treating it as a dog but recognizing it as a kindred spirit. He talked to the dog, read to the dog, and communicated with it silently, telepathically. And that is precisely what I determined to do at this critical moment. Closing my eyes, I put myself at the dogs' mercy. I sensed their presence not as mere dogs, but as living energy, residing in canine form, and capable of great good. "Cora! Woodman! Shep! Bubba! Please, do what you can!" I shouted. Then I fell silent and simply let myself feel my connection with them.

The first thing I heard was the tramp-tramp of paws over the branches near my head. Next thing I knew, Bubba, then Cora, navigated their way through the openings between the limbs and began licking my cheeks.

I could hear another of the dogs—Woodman, undoubtedly—chewing and tearing his way through branches. When he finally had a clear shot at the very tip of the trunk, he got a grip on it and tried to drag it off of me. Even for a dog of Woodman's proven talents, the task was too much. The trunk would not budge.

That's when Shep corralled Shela and Mo, who began digging out the dirt we had so recently pushed back into the hole. They managed to get beneath the branches and tunnel under the top half of my body, which soon began sinking into the re-forming hole. "My God," I thought, "am I going to be buried alive with Matt's note in this hallowed ground?" As my body dropped, it formed an incline from the spot where the trunk lay across my midsection. Woodman resumed his efforts at the tip of the trunk, and with gravity now his ally, finally managed to pull the trunk over my back and clear of my head.

At that moment, Shep herded someone else to my rescue: it was Doug. He did all the right things: cleared away the branches, knelt at my side, grabbed my trembling hand. "Emily! Are you okay?" he shrieked. "How did you get here? I can't believe I let you come down here by yourself."

"You didn't know. Doug, you'd never believe what happened here tonight. I'm not sure I believe it myself. Maybe I was in a coma and dreamed the whole thing. But it seemed like all the right dogs were down here tonight. All I need now is a St. Bernard to bring me some brandy." I tried to manage a wan smile. I looked over to see Cora, Shep, Bubba, and Woodman a few paces off, standing guard over me, their long tongues dancing as they panted heavily. Justice was there as well.

"All I want to know is, are you okay?"

All *I* wanted to know was why Matt's poem was in his coat pocket. I said nothing, but glanced over my shoulder to make sure the paper was still safely buried.

"I'll survive," I said. I paused. I knew he wanted to know something else. "I'm not so sure about the baby. My back feels like somebody pushed a lead balloon through it, all the way into my intestines. We need to get to a hospital."

At 5 a.m., the on-call GYN gave us the news I already knew. I was officially unpregnant.

As the sun came up in the hospital window, Doug shed a fair amount of tears. Enough for the both of us.

My master's sensitivity to sound and smell is much like a dog's. And I have developed a human's appreciation of sight. How lucky I am to have a master who depends on me as much as I depend on him. He holds the leash, but I lead the way. He brings me my food, but I bring him the dish in which he pours it.

— Annie

Chapter 13
Matt's Turn

The restorative benefits of time were kicking in somewhat. Actually, they were more like *trickling* in. True, I was now experiencing some isolated episodes where I'd find myself forgetting myself, living contentedly in the moment—but only for that moment.

Whiskey was no longer my constant companion. But we still enjoyed a comfortable familiarity.

One time, I did start singing in the shower. It startled me enough that I immediately stopped. I hadn't sung in the shower since last April—ten months earlier.

I was sleeping a little better. But some mornings I'd still wake up at 4 a.m. in a cold sweat from chilling dreams of Iris and Emily frolicking with S.O.S. in the mists of Doglegs.

No, I still wasn't buying into the "time heals all wounds" adage. Remember that movie, *The Story of Adele H.*? Most people don't. I do. A soldier rejects the overtures of a young woman. Instead of forgetting about him over time, her longing turns to obsession. As her pathetic existence progresses, she not only remains mad about the guy—she becomes clinically mad.

That was fiction, but we're all aware that a lot of real Adele H.'s are out there. Many of them are able to go about their lives and take care of themselves, yet something about them has changed irrevocably. They've slipped into a depression that may be invisible to the casual observer. But friends who knew them from "before" immediately sense a subtle difference that represents a sea change nonetheless. Instead of honestly experiencing a range of emotions, these walking wounded simply go through the motions. They laugh, but their laughter doesn't have the ring of authenticity. They fret, but they're not truly worried. They're just biding their time until the sweet release of death.

I was afraid I was becoming one of "them." My deep-seated optimism—my genetic birthright—had been compromised, and I was now engaged in the fight of my life, the fight *for* my life.

And I had few weapons at my disposal. Periodically, I'd try to interest myself in other women, but I found they all carried large signs that said *Not Emily*.

In such a situation, hopeless romantics like myself with enough intelligence to proactively lift themselves out of their misery might try to throw themselves into their work. But I had lost my work as well. Don't get me wrong—feeding animals is important, but it didn't engage me in the same way fixing animals did.

With Tina-Bonita gone, I would have adopted another dog—God knows, I had plenty to choose from—but I had a new landlord with a strict "no new pets" policy, so, until my lease was up, I'd be dogless.

My problem was, I didn't just like dogs. I was dog-*like*. Dogs don't experience time the way normal humans do. They aren't healed by time as easily as normal humans are. Whether you treat dogs with cruelty or affection, they don't forget it. This severely limited capacity to forget is what makes them so loyal to those they love, and I share this trait with my canine brethren. That's what kept me so closely bound to Emily. I didn't need any photographs to remember her by—the snapshots in my head had a higher resolution than anything you could achieve digitally. I didn't need a tape of her voice—her exact words rang out in my brain as clear as a bell. Like the old advertising slogan that asked, "Is it live or is it Memorex?" I almost wondered, "Is it live or is it the memory of my ex?"

Just as a good dog has only one master, I was convinced I was meant to have only one love in my life. This conviction created a sense of panic in me, because, also like a dog, I had always treasured life. I wanted to make the most of every moment. And now something—someone—had blocked me from doing that. No route was open to get me back to where I was. On bad days, I felt like Adele H. was within hailing distance. I was livin' the nightmare instead of the dream.

Still, I soldiered on. One gray Saturday morning in February, I tried to work up some enthusiasm for my bi-weekly pilgrimage to the Laundromat. Yet another charming amenity of the neighborhood, it was right next door to Biff's. Many's the time, while nursing a whiskey at Biff's, I was comforted by the whir of the washers in the spin cycle rinsing out my underwear on the other side of the wall.

Walking down the street with my basketful of clothes, I had the misfortune to pass a young couple with a baby in a stroller. Young couples with babies were especially hard on me right now, especially when they all looked as happy as these three did. God, what was wrong with me? I should have been a woman.

As I waited in the Laundromat, I amused myself by watching an elderly blind man do his wash with the help of a seeing-eye dog he called Annie. When the man missed taking a pair of shorts out of his laundry basket, Annie picked them up and put them in his hands. When he dropped one of his quarters on the floor, Annie led him to the spot where it landed.

"That's quite a dog you've got there," I said, taking a seat next to the man. The dog, a German shepherd, could have passed for Gus's sister. And once the man started talking, he could have passed for Snow White's soul brother.

"Oh, I've had lots of wonderful dogs in my time, all trying to show me the way."

"So, you've been blind from birth?"

"No, it's only been over the past three years I've lost my sight."

"This your first seeing-eye dog then?"

He turned right to me as if he could still see. "They're *all* seeing-eye dogs, every last one of 'em. And *we're all blind*. The dogs see all the things we should see, but don't. We just complicate things to the point where we can't see anything at all."

I shrugged. "You got that right."

"Back when I could see, I thought I was miserable. Hah! I used the run-down apartment that I live in as an excuse to make myself miserable. What I wouldn't give to be able to see that run-down apartment now."

"Well, you don't seem so miserable now."

"You try to change. People can change, you know, easier than dogs."

"So I've heard. How did *you* change?"

He thought about it for a moment. "Well, I suppose it was when I started thinking about the first dog I had when I was just a kid. He was an old, black cocker spaniel, and he went blind. But I remember, every time I walked into a room, even though he couldn't see me, when he heard my voice, his tail started wagging. That dog knew how to appreciate what it had. It still had its ears, and it still had me. Almost all dogs are like that. The old dogs, the sick dogs … "

"The dogs with three legs."

"Oh, definitely the ones with three legs."

"Well, I guess my load is done. But it's been nice talking to you."

And it was. He'd given me something to mull over. And as I walked back to my apartment, I was living in the moment again. Maybe it was becoming habit-forming.

Even the tedium of folding my clothes and putting them away didn't bring me down. Just as I was finishing, I heard a doorbell buzz. It gave me a start, probably because, in the four-plus months I'd lived in that apartment, this was the first time I'd heard that bell ring. Until now, I wasn't even sure that it worked. Grateful to have anybody calling on me, I buzzed them in without even asking who was there. After a minute, when nobody knocked at my door, I opened it. The only thing out there was a closed cardboard box on the floor. A closed cardboard box that made a scratching sound. Curious and curiouser.

When I opened it, a head popped out—a puppy's head, a large one, which was lucky, because it had to support a long pair of American water spaniel ears. A patch of white formed an upside-down *Y*, with the stem starting on the dog's crown and branching out around a square jaw. The rest of the dog was white with black polka dots. I couldn't stop staring at it, and I soon realized why. It was the spitting image of S.O.S. the day he jumped up on the seat next to mine on the Green Line in Boston.

As I picked him up, I felt the same shiver of anticipation I'd felt when I saw Mobile go chasing after my tennis ball on a Saturday morning in early April. Instinctively, I looked down toward the entry door beyond the foot of the stairs. There she was, half-hidden by the door's wood frame, but peeking tentatively through the edge of the glass pane.

I buzzed her in, and she stood at the bottom of the stairs, looking—well, exactly like Emily. I sensed an ironic smile trying to pop out on her face, but held back by uncertainty. And I felt déjà vu from our earlier staircase encounter, but a kind of inverse déjà vu. Now she was the one looking up.

"Is there a Matt Copeland living here?" she asked innocently.

"Yeah. I'll get him for you."

I started down the stairs and met her halfway. She hugged me so hard I was afraid she'd suffocate the puppy in my arms. I couldn't reciprocate—one, because I was holding the puppy, and two, because she was Doug's girl, and an expectant mother to boot, although I couldn't help thinking she didn't look it.

"Want to come in and take a load off your feet?" I asked, with mock-nonchalance. "We haven't talked in a while."

She nodded and followed me into my apartment without a word, yet sending out the same intimate vibe I'd felt the very first time she followed me down that trail at Doglegs. But this time it confused me. I guessed that I was mistaking her vibe for my own, that it was all a figment of my overactive imagination.

We sat down on the sofa, the puppy in my lap. I rubbed its neck, and it looked up at me in gratitude. "Is this dog for me? A peace offering?"

"The minute I saw him at the Humane Society, I knew I had to get him for you. He's just so ... so S.O.S."

"Maybe that's what I should call him: So ... S.O.S. Or just, S.O.S.O.S."

"Well, he definitely looks like the Son of Son of Sam," she said, a little too matter-of-factly.

For the first time since I'd known her, I found myself getting annoyed with Emily. "So, all of a sudden, you don't see anything wrong with that name?"

Her eyes pierced mine. "No, I don't. Not anymore. It's not important."

"You don't see *anything wrong*?" My annoyance had burst into full-blown anger. "You don't see anything wrong with giving me a puppy that could be a clone of the animal that killed Iris, and killed … us?"

The poor puppy's eyes kept darting from me to Emily back to me again. He knew something big was going on. I'm sure the dialogue was never this intense back at the Humane Society.

"Matt, I needed to give you this dog … because I needed to let you know that I've put that behind me. It was hard, Matt, but I've done it."

"I appreciate that. But I can't keep him. They don't take dogs in these apartments."

"They take dogs in *my* apartment."

"Fine. Then you keep him. He'll be a good companion for Mo."

She shook her head in frustration. "You're going to make me spell it out for you, aren't you? … Matt, I want you to come home with me."

"Huh? You and me and Doug and the baby? Oh, that's a cozy little arrangement."

Now Emily was shouting. "Matt, there's no baby anymore, dammit." Her voice and her eyes dropped together as she added, "And there's no Doug. Not for me. There's only … you."

"What? What happened? What changed for you?"

"I was blind, Matt."

"Blind." I just repeated the word, half to myself.

"Blinded by the tragedy. Punishing both of us by rejecting you—that was the only way I could deal with it. The pain of losing Iris—that won't ever go away. But I know now that I can keep you separate from that. I *have* to keep you separate from that. Things change, Matt. I've changed. I'm only human. People change."

"That's what I hear."

"What about you, Matt? Are you only human? Has everything changed for you?"

"Everything but one thing, Emily. I won't let you get away from me again," I promised. And then I sealed my promise with a kiss—maybe the sweetest, longest kiss ever. In the middle of that kiss, I started to feel her tears on my cheeks. Then I wasn't sure whose tears were whose. It was like having simultaneous orgasms. Different, but just as satisfying.

When our lips finally unlocked, I told her, "I always knew you were talented, but I had no idea anyone could kiss like that and cry like that at the same time."

"Oh, and I'll bet my eyes *aren't red*, either. And I look *extremely beautiful*." Now she was openly sobbing with joy. "Oh, Matt, I'm so sorry, for all of it."

"I am too. But to err is human."

The puppy starting licking Emily's tears, setting up her perfect comeback: "To forgive, canine."

We started laughing and crying, together.

Should my master suddenly became a monster and abuse me, I would go berserk, because I would not believe such a thing could ever be. I love him unconditionally. My identity, my well-being, are forever intertwined with his. Many dogs have sat upon this hill at their masters' sides, but in this moment, this hill is his and mine for eternity.

— Shela

Chapter 14
Doug's Turn

On a Sunday morning in April, I walked my best girl, Shela, down to Doglegs. Since the whole sordid tale had begun, one year had passed. That seemed about right. Seven dog years. The time it takes for the earth to make one complete revolution around the sun.

Now that the Dog People were coming to the woods with their dogs again, the dogs no longer felt compelled to jump fences and push aside doors in order to romp there on their own. And as I entered the woods, I noticed several innocent neophytes—new Dog People and their puppies—exploring the wonders of Doglegs. Like a forest recently ravaged by fire, Doglegs was slowly but surely renewing itself. The passage of time had lifted the curse. The rabies fear had long since subsided. The plastic-lined trash cans were fully functional. The infrastructure was back in place.

Many of the Dog People had resumed their Doglegs hikes initially because they wanted to view the fallen oak. News of Emily's ordeal and the dogs' believe-it-or-not heroics had spread through the neighborhood. The incident soon took on mythic proportions. As I approached the trunk now, which lay across my path, a boy was walking on it. The kid pretended to be a tightrope walker, doing a balancing act all the way—no matter that this trunk was more than a foot wide and resting flat on the ground. Shela, with a running start, managed to jump it, startling the boy and running smack into Woodman, busily engaged in the effort to tear off a limb.

I decided to sidestep the trunk and wandered off into the woods in the direction of the Clearing. When I got there, some of the regulars were huddled round: Greg, with Hershey and Nestle; Ben, with Justice; Snow White, who again had all Seven Arfs, having replaced her lost Yorkie.

Ben was arguing that, if Emily had been seriously hurt that night, she'd have a case against the city of Priorwood. A year before the tree fell, he explained, city workers had painted a red ring around the trunk, signaling its imminent removal as a result of severe oak wilt. "The city should have chopped down that tree last summer," he said. I wished I could have asked him whether a lost fetus—and a lost relationship—were grounds for legal action.

Steering the conversation in a more positive direction, Greg starting talking about the proposal to put up a plaque in the woods commemorating the events that transpired during the Night of the Falling Oak. "Hell, I could work on that. Now that I've finally cleaned up the backlog of shit around here, I've got some time on my hands."

Elaine and Woodman approached the Clearing from the north, arriving just as Marie and Shep crisscrossed their path from the south. The two women's courtroom battle over Marie's fall into the ditch had not been pretty. As they passed each other now, each acted as though the other were invisible. Not a glimmer of acknowledgment registered on either face.

No, Doglegs did not feel like its old self. It felt like its new self. It had reclaimed its relevance, but relinquished its innocence. No longer was this place sealed off from the real world—it was simply a microcosm of it. Maybe with time things would revert back to the good old days. On the other hand, maybe the good old days weren't so good.

Ben and Greg headed out, leaving Snow White and myself in the Clearing. I saw Emily and Matt approaching from the second dogleg, and I was determined to stand my ground, if only because they had seen that I saw them.

They were smiling, chatting, joking. Disgusting.

Matt greeted us with an isn't-life-wonderful, "Hi, guys."

"Hey," I replied.

"Another beautiful day in the neighborhood," chimed in Snow White.

Emily just smiled this funny, frozen smile. She and Matt kept right on walking.

161

The dogs were the only ones who didn't appear awkward, whose actions didn't seem forced. Mobile jumped up, gave my face one quick lick, then ran off with their new dog, a dead ringer for S.O.S.

Shela ran after Matt and Emily, did a little dance around them, then came back and lay down at my feet.

"Not the best of times for you, are they, Doug?" Snow White observed.

I nodded. Most anyone else saying those particular words at that particular time, I'd call nosy. Snow White I called all-knowing.

"Who was he kidding, moving off to Morrissey? Pretending to be this suffering martyr. Getting into brawls. That's not in his nature. It was all a ploy to win Emily back. And I've got to hand it to him—it worked. He even got the Veterinary Board to rescind his license suspension. Yeah, everything is just lollipops and roses for them right now."

"If it's any consolation," she replied, "they won't always be as happy together as they are right now."

"What are you saying? You don't think it'll last?"

"Oh, it very well might. Maybe they're made for each other. But it still won't be a bed of roses. It never is. If it's a bed of roses you're looking for, you've got your perfect partner." She waved her hand down toward Shela, looking like a perfect angel at my feet. "Remember this, Doug: 'Dogs love their friends and bite their enemies, quite unlike people, who are incapable of pure love and always have to mix love and hate.'"

"Molly, you say the most profound stuff sometimes."

She chuckled. "That wasn't a Snow White original, Doug. That one I borrowed from Sigmund Freud."

"I'm sure it sounds better coming from you. But ya know, Molly, Freud was right. Part of me hates Matt and Emily, part of me wants to go tagging along after them right now. I love them both. I'm almost willing to let Matt be the alpha male in order to rejoin their pack."

"So what's stopping you?"

"The hate part." Molly didn't know about Emily's pregnancy. She didn't know that Matt and Emily's bond was indirectly responsible for my unborn child remaining unborn. And she didn't know that Emily's official breakup with me was a pretty bad scene.

Still, Molly knew enough—enough to provide a spot-on diagnosis "You feel anger and shame and guilt and pride."

"I guess. All that good stuff. Matt and I always played these games of one-upmanship. But all of a sudden, the stakes got too high. I lost everything—my girl, my friend … my self-respect."

"Maybe you can win a little bit back."

"How do you mean?"

"You can show them you're a better loser than he was."

"Ya think?"

"Yes, I do. You're the man."

I didn't need any more convincing. For one instant, I locked eyes with Molly, then dashed off to catch up with my erstwhile playmates.

When I did, they were already out of the woods, at the edge of Webster Field. My, "Hey!" got them to turn around and stop. For a long moment, we stood there silently. I had no planned speech, but then the words just came. "I don't know about you guys, but I can't pass you by and just

163

keep walking. It's uncomfortable. It's unnatural. So I've got two options. I could stop coming down to Doglegs altogether. But that doesn't appeal to me, and it sure-as-hell wouldn't sit well with Shela. So that leaves option two: beg you to let bygones be bygones. The thing is, not only do I miss you both, but I think I like the two of you better when you're together than when you're apart. And I have a hunch you're gonna be together a long time."

Matt and Emily gave each other a knowing look. Then Emily indicated the tennis ball in her hand and brought her arm up into throwing position. "Alright, guys ... on the count of three. And I want to see some hustle. One ... two ... two-and-a-half ... three."

Emily got a strong throw off, and away we went. I pushed Matt to the side, and he pushed me. For a moment, we were twelve-year-olds again. We reached the ball in a dead heat and dived for it. I landed on Matt, Matt landed on the ball. With ball in hand, he raised his arm and waved it back and forth, letting Emily know who the victor was.

As Emily came up to rejoin us, we noticed that Shela, Mobile, and Matt's new dog came with her. "Were they with you the whole time?" Matt asked.

"Yep."

"Humph! And they didn't go for the ball," I added.

"Nope. I think they realized this game was just for you guys."

We all smiled. Emily's icebreaker had worked, up to a point.

"Doug, I'm glad you made the first move," Matt said. "That took balls." He tossed me the tennis ball.

"Well, somebody had to do it. I da man."

"We'd like you to come over for dinner tonight," Emily offered.

"We would?" Matt asked, eyeing Emily. "We would."

Emily continued, without missing a beat. "And if you'd like to bring—"

"Oh, I'm not seeing anybody."

"I mean, you should bring Shela."

"Absolutely. Shela's always up for a home-cooked meal."

We laughed, nervously. As the conversation had progressed, or regressed, we found ourselves hampered by the inevitable mood-killing thoughts: the "I-wonder-what-she's-thinkings," the "hope-they-don't-take-that-the-wrong-way's," the "things-seem-weird-and-will never-get-back-to-how-they-used-to-be's." We were hamstrung by all the self-conscious crap that makes us work so hard to secure something with humans that we get with dogs naturally: honest companionship.

I gave them each a quasi-heartfelt hug and wandered back into the woods with Shela. What I felt more than anything at that moment was relief.

Three-quarters of the way down the second dogleg, I had a chance encounter. The chance of my life, it seemed. I had never seen a woman like this. Maybe once or twice, but never like this—at Doglegs, with no one else around, except her and me and our dogs.

"Hi. Haven't seen you in these woods before."

"I just moved into the neighborhood."

"Cool."

"What a great place for dog-walking. Do you come here often?"

"Twice a day."

"Great. We'll look forward to seeing you. What kind of dog is that? She's beautiful."

"Shela? … she's a Lab-shepherd mix." Oh God, how I ached to cut the bull and get down to business. "Listen, I was wondering, if you're around tomorrow night—"

"Oh, tomorrow night my partner and I have a ton of unpacking to do."

"Your partner?"

"Here she comes now. Jamie," she called out, "come meet our new friend."

Preceded by her Irish setter, Jamie made her entrance into the woods via the path coming down from the ridge. She had short hair, black-rimmed glasses, baggy clothes, and, like partner number one, beauty out of the ordinary. If Julia Roberts played the part of an intellectual lesbian, they would make her up to resemble Jamie. Shit.

After all the requisite hellos and goodbyes, Shela and I made our way up the ridge. When we reached the top, with Eden View Park stretched out before us, I didn't see a soul, very unusual for a Sunday morning. I lay down on the freshly green Eden View slope, and Shela nuzzled up next to me. God, I love that dog.

Closing my eyes, I thought about the tumultuous year past. Doglegs had taken Matt and Emily to hell and back. Life had its winners and losers. Right now, Matt and Emily looked like winners, as much as anyone can in this world. The lives of human beings are pretty damn unpredictable though. I wasn't about to venture any guesses as to whether they—or I—would ultimately land in the winners' camp.

But lying there, with the sun beating down on me and a good dog at my side, I felt bulletproof. I'll bet we looked like a fucking Norman Rockwell painting.

Printed in the United States
by Baker & Taylor Publisher Services